TWO
FOR THE
PAIN

AN EDDIE GIDEON MYSTERY

JAMES MOORER

DARK ANTHEM PRESS

Copyright © 2016, 2022, 2024 by James Moorer

All rights reserved.

This book is entirely a work of fiction. Any references to real events, real people, or real places are used fictitiously. Other names, characters, places, and events are products of the author's imagination. Any resemblance to actual events, places, or persons, living or dead, is entirely coincidental. No artificial intelligence (A.I.) or predictive language software was used in any part of the creation of this book.

No portion of this book may be reproduced in any form without written permission from the publisher or author, except as permitted by U.S. copyright law. It is illegal to copy this book, post it to a website, or distribute it by any other means without permission. The author expressly prohibits using this work in any manner for purposes of training artificial intelligence technologies to generate text, including without limitation, technologies that are capable of generating works in the same style or genre as this work. The author reserves all rights to license uses of this work for generative AI training and development of machine learning language models.

Created and printed in the United States of America.

Third edition, 2024

Published by Dark Anthem Press, an imprint of One Moorer LLC.

Identifiers: 979-8-9911025-5-1 (hardcover) | 979-8-9911025-7-5 (ebook) | 979-8-9911025-6-8 (paperback) | 979-8-9911025-8-2 (audiobook)

Subjects: *Mystery & Detective*—Fiction | *Suspense*—Fiction | *Thrillers*—Fiction | *Crime*—Fiction |

Dedicated to my aunt Emma Jean Henry, whose library of books was my childhood gateway to imagination.

ONE

"**G**et up!" the man startled me awake.

Nothing aggravates me more than someone awakening me from a sound sleep. I consider it a criminal, intrusive act deserving of every expletive known to man. I never liked it as a child, when my mother gently rustled me from dreams of riding on the range. I hated it when my ex-wife yanked me about like a mop handle mere seconds before the alarm would sound. Imagine my aggravation when three strangers came calling, armed with guns and a great deal of attitude.

My name is Eddie Gideon. To most of my friends, I'm Gitz, and no one in their right mind or with a poor dental plan makes fun of my name. I'm thirty-eight, divorced and in good health, with no desire to bear any of the politically correct, hyphenated cultural distinctions that appear to be in fashion these days. I'm a Black man, plain and simple.

I live alone, work hard, and occasionally enjoy the company of a lady or two when time allows. I've been threatened, beaten up, and shot. These are normal occurrences in the life of a private investigator. It's a tough line of work and I wouldn't recommend it to anyone who digs the nine to five. The hours are long and a pension plan is something I've only daydreamed about from time to time. I do get to meet people, travel, and carry a gun. Occasionally life surprises me, sometimes just by waking to another day. Waking up to guns in my face was something I never expected to happen.

"I said get up! Put your hands—"

Instinct and years of training kicked in, and my right leg rose from beneath the sheets. I drove my heel into the man's jaw on my right. I was already sitting upright when his partner, a cop, barked at me with his gun just inches from my face.

"Stop right there!"

Naked, unarmed, and embarrassed, I did as he instructed. It isn't every morning I wake up with some guy shaking a gun at me, but that doesn't mean I'm about to just roll over and ignore him, either. I didn't care for the way his hands trembled.

Two cops flanked each side of the double bed while the third struggled to get off the floor.

"Keep your hands where I can see them. Move slowly," the one on my right shouted at me.

The momentary adrenaline was beginning to fade. I moved sluggishly. Everything happened so fast that my head wouldn't stop spinning. I detected a sickening sweet taste in my mouth, which I didn't remember from the night before. My eyes darted between cops, as my mind raced to figure out what the hell was happening. The cop to my left squinted behind his wire-rimmed spectacles. His face seemed familiar—round and puffy, like a gingerbread man.

I paid close attention to the cop moving in front of me. He couldn't have been over twenty-four. Tall and lean in the face, he had tiny freckles to match his orange hair. His long arms hung awkwardly, as though they belonged to someone else. He looked apprehensive; a bit unsure of himself. The third guy hobbled onto his feet and limped out of the room, holding his jaw.

Then I remembered I hadn't spent the night alone. I was with someone, a woman. Carole. Where did Carole go? Did she let the police in? Why were they giving me such a hard time? My mouth and brain struggled to synchronize as a rush of coldness enveloped me. I spun around, peering back at the bed. I'd gone to sleep with Carole lying next to me, catching the smell of her skin, opening my eyes once or twice to watch her as she slept. She lay there all night beside me, her warmth like a blanket against my skin. Now the sight of her left me cold. A tiny red stream of blood ran from the center of her chest to the base of her throat. Her black hair fell over her face like overgrown grass covering a stone. I reached out to brush back the long strands. Her eyes stared back at me, blank and lifeless.

"Get away from the body!" The cop shouted again.

"Just take it easy." I raised my hands in plain sight.

"Shut up, rat-fink!"

Something about that rodent reference struck a familiar nerve. The cop to my left moved next to his partner, and a sickening realization washed over me. I didn't recognize him earlier because Barney Sampson had put on some weight since I last saw him. Although the uniform was larger, one thing about him hadn't changed. He hated my guts.

"Barney. Can I have my pants?" I pointed down at the floor.

"Think you can get them on while wearing these?" He waved his handcuffs in front of me. He frowned when I shook my head in response. "You're in a lot of trouble, Gideon."

"Jeez, Barney, you know this guy?"

"Eddie Gideon," Barney said through gritted teeth, "He used to be somebody once."

Barney reached down and lifted my pants with two fingers. After his careful inspection, he threw them in my direction. His partner appeared clueless, unsure of what to do. His dumbfounded expression made him look even more like a kid. Poor bastard. Bad enough the department saddled him with a bigoted asshole like Barney, but then to go out on a call like this? He couldn't stop shaking. Sweat poured out of him so fast you'd have thought he was bleeding.

"I used to be a cop." I drew my pants up over my knees.

"Bullshit." Barney stuck his finger in my face. "You were never one of us."

I rose, ignoring Barney's comments, and pulled up my pants. My head felt as though someone had kicked it repeatedly for laughs. I glanced back at his partner again. I don't think I ever took my eyes off of him. It amazed me he hadn't blown chunks all over the place or that I hadn't fallen apart right then and there. I read his name tag, Marren. I tried smiling at him, hoping to make him relax, go easy a bit.

"This isn't what it looks like."

"Yeah, right." Barney kicked what he mistook for my shirt in my direction. "Why don't you tell us what it is, bro?"

"You're a real funny guy," I bent down slowly. "By the way, this is a blouse."

"What's the matter, not your shade?"

Any other time, I'd have knocked him square on his ass. But Barney wanted me to do something stupid, to give him a reason to cut loose on me. He didn't have the brains I gave him credit for.

I stood up again. "My shirt's on the other side of the bed."

"Tough shit." Barney clamped the cuffs on my wrist. "You'll get a shirt in the hole."

Barney pulled my arm behind me while Marren read me my rights. All I could do was stare at the body of Carole Spenser. I tried to remember the last time I heard her voice, felt her move against me. I tried to focus my thoughts, wondering how this had happened with me right there next to her on the bed. The last thing I remember was falling asleep with her cradled in my arms, the warmth of our bodies igniting the senses, like lightning arcing across the night sky.

What the fuck happened here? Someone murdered Carole. How did they find out? Who called them? Why didn't I hear them when they kicked the door in? The thoughts pressed against my brain, like a child's persistent tapping.

"Didn't think murder was quite your style," Barney steered me towards the door. "Why'd you kill the broad?"

"I didn't kill anyone."

"You're not one of those freaks into bangin' dead broads?" Barney stammered. "God, that makes me sick."

He opened the door and guided me out. The sudden chill of the morning air hit me hard, shaking me back to reality. Four more cops were waiting as Barney shoved me into the cruiser.

"Okay Hicks, we got 'em! Call for a bus. We've got a corpse inside." Barney rattled off his commands, pointing and directing like a symphony conductor.

Marren came running, just steps behind us, and threw my shirt and shoes in next to me as Barney shut the door. Barney walked to the other officers and spoke with them. Their glares revealed that he told them my identity.

Marren returned to the car, made sure to properly secure me, then slid into the front seat.

"I'm telling the truth. I didn't kill her." I leaned forward.

"It's best you remain quiet, sir."

"Don't you think if I'd have done it, I'd be long gone instead of lying there waiting for you guys to bust my ass?"

"I don't know, sir."

This sir crap was getting on my nerves. But then, his nerves resembled spaghetti right now. "Marren, I'm just trying to help us both. Common sense should tell you that something about all of this stinks, or don't you care?"

He turned and gave me an incredulous look, but then his eyes drifted. He wondered, but only for a second, about what he'd seen. "Did you really used to be a cop? One of us?"

Just as I prepared to latch onto the doubt in his voice, the door opened and Barney Sampson slipped behind the wheel. He'd caught the tail end of our conversation.

"Don't mess with this guy, kid. He's a blemish on the department and a disgrace to the uniform." Barney started the car. "Not to mention a cold-blooded killer."

"I told you I didn't kill anyone."

"Yeah," he turned to me, "Somebody sure as hell turned her into a popsicle. If you didn't, then who the hell did, huh?"

Damn good question. Even as we pulled away, I didn't have an answer, not for them or for myself. I couldn't make sense of anything that was happening around me. My head felt like someone had teed off with a sledgehammer. Despite the cool morning air, sweat rolled down my back. I sat there, hands cuffed behind me, thinking of the woman I'd made love to last night. The first woman I'd told "I love you" in seven years. I fought back the urge to weep like a child. I clenched my teeth and tried to hang on to my sanity, tried to damp the rage threatening to consume me. I had to put aside my pain.

I needed to be silent, keep it together. Losing it now wouldn't bring her back, any more than it would help me. Somehow, someone had come in and killed her right under my very nose. That thought didn't sit well with me. It wouldn't sit any better with the police, either. I wasn't exactly at the top of their Christmas card list for various reasons. Before reaching the station, I had to find a way to make them understand.

Sirens wailed as we turned onto the main drag heading south. Cars moved aside, curious to catch a glimpse of me as we sailed by. I tried to immerse myself in the noise, the trumpeting call of trouble. With the way things had unfolded, it could have easily been Gabriel's horn sounding. I knew what the next few hours would bring for me, and all signs pointed to one chilling conclusion: all hell was about to break loose.

TWO

As we headed into the city on state route 315, the morning sun warmed my bare skin. They were taking me directly downtown for processing. Barney kept making stupid jokes, and Marren looked like he'd puke at any minute. I leaned back and tried to make myself as comfortable as possible. My fingers tingled from the lack of circulation to my hands. But my mind wasn't on my hands or the stupid riddle Barney tried to explain to Marren for the third time. My thoughts remained with the woman we'd left lying naked and cold on her bed, murdered for reasons I still couldn't piece together. I ached for a touch I'd never feel again. Her kiss was now lost to me forever.

Four months ago I met a woman, and I mean woman in every sense of the word. Carole Spenser, a stylish and self-assured stockbroker, quickly became an important part of my life. I readily made plans for how we'd be spending the next few weeks, or at least the next morning. Presumptuous as hell, but I deserved a little high school fantasy. Besides, what did I have to lose by dreaming? But that was before last night.

Yesterday had been one of those endless and irritating days. I turned down a case from a guy who suspected his wife of cheating on him. He wanted me to dig up the dirt so he could screw her in the settlement. I never take cases like that. A little too close to home. For the most part, I lived a mundane life. Nothing much more exciting than an occasional run-in with my ex-wife Cassandra, the most beautiful pain-in-the-ass I knew. My office and apartment were located in a two-story brownstone off High Street, above Deacon's. My best friend John Deacon owned the best little nightclub in Short North, a renovated area of art galleries, clothing shops, and bistros just north of downtown Columbus, Ohio. In the last few years, the two-mile stretch had become the fashionable place to hang out. Even with the nearby Easton Towne Center, the trendy set preferred the intimacy of North's atmosphere. John had been lucky enough to get the place for a reasonable rate before the big renovation surge swept through the run-down area and skyrocketed the rents of the storefront properties. I made it my usual hangout when I finished work, most convenient to simply walk downstairs.

The place exuded a timeless charm with its polished hardwood floors, neon fixtures in the windows, abundant brass, and a vintage Coca-Cola machine. There was usually a girl sitting just past the door, ready to take customers' coats and hang them on the shiny brass hooks behind her. At the right side of the building, rows of tables draped in dark blue linen separated the bar from the sound stage.

Deacon's was one of the few places in town where you could still hear real music played by real people. People flocked from near and far to listen to whichever band or jazz musician happened to be in town. No one on earth knew more people in the music business than John Deacon. It wasn't unusual for the local radio stations to reach out to John about which hot talent would make a surprise appearance at his place.

As my day ended, I took my usual stroll downstairs. Deacon spotted me at the door and waved me up to the bar, assessing my mood before I said a word.

John Deacon had a body like Arnold Schwarzenegger—wide chest, cut to the max—despite being just a year older than me. He was like a Brahma Bull, towering over others with his thick shoulders. But John was a sweetheart, the kind of guy everyone wants as their friend. He had this way of drawing people to him, if not with his chiseled features, certainly with the way he played the alto sax.

"Deac, where's the liquor?" I held up my glass.

"You got the standard pour, Gitz." He turned to put the bottle back on the shelf. "Scotch isn't going to help your problem, anyway."

I knew what he meant before I asked. "And what problem might that be, my brother?"

"You've been seeing this Carole now for quite a few months. Is it something serious or what?" he grinned.

"You think I'm rushing in too fast?" I ran my finger along the rim of the glass.

"Maybe." He poured himself a soda. "Though it's nice not to see you down-in-the-mouth over something Cassandra's done to you. It's good to see you up for a change."

"Nice to know you're looking out for me." I sipped my scotch.

"How come you still get all bent out of shape over Cassandra, anyway? You've been divorced for a long time."

"Maybe I'd grown accustomed to her bark. She could be a bitch, but she was—"

"—Gitz, don't you dare!" a woman's voice behind me interrupted. A perky little redhead bounced to the bar. Rita Harold, one of John's better cocktail waitresses. She served as the resident love counselor and psychic advisor, and she was also sweet.

"Don't you dare sink to her level. You've got too pure a spirit to succumb like that." She shook her finger at me.

"Why thank you, Rita." I raised my glass to her. "It's not often a woman says something so nice to me."

Deacon flashed her a not-so-nice look and Rita scurried back to her tables.

Later, as our well-worn Browns vs. Broncos debate was in full swing, Carole approached the bar. Her complexion was a beautiful honey brown and her lips were full and alluring. Standing at about five foot seven, Carole had the kind of figure that was famous for stopping traffic. The cinnamon scent of her perfume arrived just slightly before she did. She leaned up against the bar, not sitting down yet. Then she turned toward the bandstand, staring out into the crowd. She was absolutely stunning. Her long black hair bounced across her shoulders. Her high cheekbones were accentuated by expressive highlights. Quietly, she slid next to me, revealing a long black seam that gently touched her calf and extended up her thigh, disappearing under her tweed skirt.

"Hi Deacon. Scotch and water, please." She slid a twenty in front of her and threw me a casual glance.

"Sure thing, Carole." Deacon smiled and dropped a cocktail napkin next to the twenty.

"Ready for another, Gitz?" he asked.

"Gitz. Now there's an interesting name." She pretended not to know me.

Interesting name? Every time I heard those words, I'd get this twinge from my jaw to my eyebrows. I didn't care for those words, especially when it came to my name. But I responded politely, playing along. "It's a family name. My father gave it to me."

"My grandfather used to call me Carolina. I think he did it just to piss my parents off." She smiled as she sat down.

I played along as if we were meeting for the first time. "What did you call him?"

Her eyes fell away from me, like someone had just whispered in her ear. A look of remembrance flashed across her face. The way she smiled made me think of a child's expression when riding a pony on a merry-go-round for the very first time. Her eyes came up to me again.

"I called him Cappie."

"My name's Eddie Gideon." I re-introduced myself.

"Carole Spenser." She shook my hand. "Can I buy you a drink?"

"Don't take this the wrong way, but shouldn't I be buying you a drink?"

"A gentleman too." She laughed. "You're a rare find these days, Mr. Gideon. What are you doing for the rest of the evening?"

We ended our little game with a kiss, actually several kisses. We soon left for a showing of her favorite movie, "Imitation of Life," starring Lana Turner and Susan Kohner. One could only guess what drew Carole to this film, or why, after seeing it as many times as we had, it always brought her to tears. Something about that film moved Carole in a way I didn't understand.

Carol had come to Columbus from Chicago six months ago. She fell in love with the city from day one. In the four months we had spent together, Carole became my friend, lover, and confidant. She was a breath of fresh air in my otherwise whiskey colored life. I had all but given up on any relationship when she found me browsing through a bookstore. Though I'd spotted her before she noticed me, Carole made the first move. Suddenly life seemed pleasant, almost tolerable with her filling the gaps, giving me back what my divorce had taken out of me.

After the movie, we went for a drive out by Hoover Dam. I loved the way she laughed, so cheerful and bubbly. Now and then I felt the urge to say something stupid like, "Where have you been all my life?" or "I've waited my whole life for someone like you," but my mouth just wasn't up to the task. An hour later, we stood in front of her condo in Arlington Hills.

"Can I be direct with you, Eddie?" She leaned so close I could feel her breath upon me. "I know we've been together four months, but it's a big deal that I'm letting you inside my place. It's highly unusual for me."

"I'm not making any presumptions, if you're wondering." I whispered sheepishly.

She smiled again. "Still the gentleman and so incredibly handsome, too." She pressed her lips against mine, then slowly pulled away. "Come in. There's something I want you to see."

I decided not to guess what she meant. My heart pounded so fast I could hardly think, anyway. She slipped out of her pumps as she glided across the room. The living room had a minimalist style, with black and white colors dominating the decor. Ty Wilson prints decorated the walls—twin portraits of dark subtle stokes against a white canvas, each of a lover's embrace. The modular furnishings gave a dynamic, picturesque presentation. So I've learned from watching PBS.

"Real nice place." I complemented her.

"Can I get you something?" She moved from one room to another. An article of clothing dropped as she passed by.

"No thanks, I'm fine." I felt like a schoolboy out past curfew.

Suddenly, I wondered what she was looking for. Spiked heels, a pair of handcuffs? Maybe I could run home and get mine? It came as a pleasant surprise when she stood in the doorway shadowed in a black teddy, honey brown skin shimmering against the soft folds. She motioned me to follow her deeper into the apartment, back to the bedroom.

She pointed down at the bed. "Four months we've been together and we've never done it in this bed. We've never done it in this apartment. Can you believe it?" She sat on the corner.

"Could be the mattress." I offered dryly.

"No, it's fine. Come see." She patted the pale blue comforter that dressed the bed.

My throbbing heart rang in my ears like a twenty-one-gun salute. She grabbed my hand just as I touched the sheets. Her eyes strayed around the room for a moment, and then she laughed. A tear glistened in her eye and Carole put her hand over her face to hide her embarrassment.

"I'm sorry," she said finally. "I just can't believe I'm doing this. It's not like me at all." She seemed close to tears.

"Would you like me to leave?" I really didn't want to.

"Oh no, please stay." She squeezed my hand. "I'm just really caught up in what I'm feeling right now. I'm not so good when it comes to trying to keep things in perspective. I never felt this way about another man. I've never tried so hard to impress anyone in my life. I don't know why it's so hard for me."

Carole didn't have to finish for me to understand what she was trying to say. She wrapped her arms around herself. I found myself looking at her as though seeing her for the first time.

"Carole, you know I think you're pretty special. And I can't say I've always said what was on my mind all the time." I reached out and stroked her cheek with my hand. "But you must have guessed by now that it's been just as hard for me to tell you how I feel, not knowing what to say or how you'll respond once I've said it."

She stared at me. "Can we believe in fairy tales? Can love survive when all else fails?"

I smiled. "A poem you wrote?"

She shook her head. "Streisand, 'My Heart Belongs to Me.' I don't know why, but that just suddenly popped into my head."

I took her hand. "Maybe you're trying to tell yourself that there's room enough inside of you for two hearts, that there's room enough for the both of us."

"So, what do we do now?" A tear glistened on her cheek.

"Right now, we don't have to say a word. We don't have to think about what is or isn't going to happen tomorrow. Now is all we have to care about. Whatever happens tomorrow, we have the best of one another tonight."

Carole drew closer to me as her fingers rested against my lips. I suckled them in earnest. Then I plunged my tongue deeply into her mouth before she could utter another word. Her warm ambrosia skin tasted sweet, giving off a static charge that made my thighs tingle, my hands hungry for every part of her. We fell against the perfumed sheets, our lips wrestling at a sweeping pace, fingers pulling and caressing all at once.

The moment felt intoxicating, everything about her so right. Beautiful, smart, funny, and she *was* with me tonight. I tried not to delude myself, let my passion lead me to say something she wasn't ready to hear, or I myself wasn't committed enough to say. But I had fallen in love with her. And if she didn't know it, she soon would.

"Carole." I called her name, "I love you."

THREE

Columbus, Ohio. It's not the most glamorous city for a private investigator, but then you'd be surprised at what went on in the Midwest. Compared to any of the big towns, when it came to sleaze and slander, we ranked. Sure, there are nice, quiet, peaceful little communities scattered all about; but like they used to say about kids in school, it's the quiet ones you have to watch out for.

Police headquarters had changed several times in the years I'd lived in this city. It had gone from a small brick building the size of an elementary school to a glass and stone tower, cutting into the sky like a dagger above Marconi Boulevard. The place looked more like a corporate headquarters for some multi-million-dollar company. But in this town, that seemed to fit.

I worked out of homicide for six years and, despite the way my career as a cop ended, it was the best time of my life. Most of who I am remains locked within those corridors; in the squad room where I listened dutifully to Sergeant Bates at roll call; in the gym trying to talk over Irv Bingham's loud radio; on the wooden bench that too often became a bed on nights when filing the paperwork took forever. The names and faces changed along with the paint on the walls. But even the best paint peels occasionally to let the pale, chalky olive-colored past come to the surface again.

Now I had returned, back in homicide, in a world of shit, and quite certain a few select cops in the precinct would jump at the chance to flush me into oblivion. Maybe because of the way I had treated some of the bad apples. I never hid that I despised cops who thought their badges made them superior. Maybe because of the way things went down when I left the force.

Police scandals are hard to live down. No one wanted to hear about a cop shooting some kid in cold blood to cover up the fact he and a couple of his buddies took drugs from dealers, only to turn around and sell the shit themselves. They only remember a cop ratting out his buddies, betraying a sacred code to do the right thing. I got screwed then, and I had a feeling someone was trying to screw me now. Only a few friendly faces greeted me as I gave my statement to the arresting officers. One belonged to Lieutenant Louis Brandon.

At fifty-something, Lou had a stocky build with rugged features. His stone washed complexion looked pale under the eyes. The streaks of grey in his sideburns were like a sergeant's stripes. He had the eyes of a man who breathed only second-hand air and stole his sleep in minutes.

"What the hell have you gotten yourself into now, Gitz?" He leaned in my direction. "What's this about a murder?"

"I'm trying to put the pieces together myself," I said.

"You better put them together, real fast. I hear the D.A.'s office has already caught wind of this and you know what that means." He rubbed his temples. "You don't need that kind of heat."

The District Attorney had no love for me. "Nelson's probably doing somersaults in his office right now." I sighed. "How'd the D.A.'s office get word so fast?"

"They've got friends like everyone else." He glanced around the room. "Nelson has eyes and ears in the department and in an election year, everybody wants to be pals with all the right people. So who got killed?"

"A very special lady." I tried to suppress the image of Carole dead in her bed. "Somebody who didn't deserve to die that way."

"You really look like shit, Gitz. Your timing couldn't have been worse," he grunted.

"Like I give a fuck about how lousy my timing is," I fumed. "Look, I fell asleep with her in my arms and I woke up to two-and-a-half cops pointing weapons in my face."

Lou shrugged. "You didn't see or hear anything?"

"If I did, she'd be alive, or I'd be dead too."

"Maybe whoever killed her used a silencer."

"Doubtful, even at close range. You know any cops or former cops who sleep that soundly?"

The reality of that fact stung me more than I cared to admit. Some things you learn in life become second nature, like breathing. I have never been a sound sleeper. Even as a kid, when old man Martin would come tipping in across the street from one of his late-night binges, I could count the number of times he'd drop his keys. As a cop, my training taught me to never let my guard down and pay attention to things most people take for granted. For fun, we used to take bets in the locker rooms on what kind of gun a guy had just from listening to it being cocked. I could look at a knife wound and tell you whether the perpetrator was right-handed or left-handed. No way could I have slept through a murder.

Lou and I watched the young officer as he yanked his completed report from the printer. I must have been his first collar, judging from the gleam in his eye. He looked pleased as punch to have his lieutenant standing by to see him in action.

"I'll go over your report later, Marren. You did a fine job." Lou gave him the congratulatory brush-off.

"Lieutenant, I can take the suspect down to holding—"

"That won't be necessary, Marren." Lou said. "I'll take it from here. He'll remain in my custody."

"But sir, I—"

"—You what, Marren?"

Marren got the message and took off. Lou leaned against the edge of his desk and crossed his arms. He peered down at me with a stern, fatherly look, squinting as though he wasn't sure if he really knew the person who sat before him.

"This is the third time in so many months I've had to cover your ass, Gitz. I'm really going out on a limb here for you."

"Lou, you know I wouldn't do something like this," I said.

"I know you wouldn't kill anybody without a good reason, Gitz." He sounded like the damned D.A. himself.

I threw him an icy stare, wondering where he found the balls to even ask. "You know better. You know me better than that."

Lou patted me on the back. "Pray the prosecutor's office is as easily convinced as I am, Gitz. You're gonna need all the help you can get."

"Then help me get the real killer, Lou. I want whoever did this." I gritted my teeth.

"How do you plan to do that?"

"Maybe if I could get back in her apartment, try to put together the pieces of what happened there last night."

He shook his head. "No way Gitz, that's a crime scene."

"And I just happen to be accused of that crime." I said. "If there is any proof of my guilt or innocence, it's in that apartment."

"I can't let you go back in there. The D.A.'s office would be all over us," he snapped.

"Fuck him. It's my ass on the line, not his."

Lou threw up his hands. "Just like that? Fuck the D.A.? Fuck departmental procedure, and fuck everybody?"

"The place will be full of cops—homicide, vice, forensics, and the M.E. You can keep the cuffs on me if it makes you feel better. Stand guard over me the whole time we're there. All I'm asking you to do is help me try to clear myself."

He laughed. "You're some piece of work, Gitz. You get busted for your girlfriend's murder, picked up at the crime scene, and after I save the taxpayers a few dollars by keeping you outta jail, you still want me to bend over some, huh, and not so much as kiss before you hump me, right?"

"I'm not asking you to kiss my ass, Lou, just help me save it, alright?" I replied.

He frowned. "Why should I?"

"What the fuck do you mean, why? You're a police officer, for Pete's sake. Because I'm your friend and Stephie would never forgive her Uncle Lou for not helping me." I hit him below the belt.

"Leave Stephie out of this!" His finger jabbed the air in front of my nose. "If you had spent more time trying to be a better father to her, you might not be in this mess."

I sighed. "Are we gonna screw around all day or what?"

Lou shoved his hands in his pockets and stared down at me, his eyes bulging like two over-ripe grapes. He pulled out a key for the handcuffs and removed them from my wrists.

"It's a good thing that kid's special to me, Gitz," he grunted.

"Then be a good uncle and get your coat."

I felt like a genuine piece of shit for using my own kid to get my way with Lou. He had no children of his own, and when Cassandra and I first got married, he became the father-in-law I thought I'd left in Maryland. He adored Stephie, and she wasn't above using good old Uncle Lou to help her get anything she wanted. "Uncle Lou says I'm old enough to ride a motorcycle. Uncle Lou thinks I'm mature enough to have my own phone." Uncle Lou could be a pain in the ass when he felt like it.

***

It was well past noon when we arrived. The sunny day had darkened into gray, and the rain poured in buckets. Lou had been kind enough to take me home to change clothes and grab my trench coat. The forensics team had already started working when we got back to Carole's apartment. These boys were meticulous, careful not to let anything slip by their probing eyes, fingers, and, in some cases, their noses. The four-man team buzzed about the townhouse like a bunch of kids digging to find the prize at the bottom of a Cracker Jack box. The only familiar face came from the medical examiner's office.

Skip Butler stood in the bedroom's doorway and waved us over. Skip had just turned thirty a week ago. His long black hair was pulled into a ponytail. He wore a white lab coat over his Bauhaus T-shirt and tattered jeans, which did little to hide that he was lanky and bowlegged. Skip bopped his head to the earbuds in his ears. His musical taste was pretty avant-garde for his age. He was heavy into classic post-punk, alternative groups like The Cure, Skinny Puppy, Front 242, and Depeche Mode. Music I never acquired a taste for.

"Isn't there a joke about something like this somewhere?" Skip moved one earbud from his ear to his lab coat pocket, music blaring like a trumpet. "Gee, Gitz, you look like hell."

He was right. On any other day, the dark cloud I woke up with would have passed by now. But I felt worse as the day dragged on. My shirt clung to me from all the sweat. I felt like I had a burning fever.

"Lieutenant Brandon, awfully nice to have a high-ranking official drop by to see us civil servants hard at work," Skip said.

"I know a barber with a hard-on for you, son," Lou returned the sarcasm with a dirty look. "You got anything for us yet?"

Skip strolled around the bed where Carole and I had spent the night making love.

I could taste her, still catch a breath of her scent upon me. The room was still ardent with our humid passion. The wrinkled sheets where our bodies wrestled at a fevered pitch were now soaked with her blood.

Skip stood at the side of the bed where Carole had lain and shook his head. "Looks like we got one strange murder here."

"How do you mean?" I frowned at him.

"Well, first of all, from the smell of the place, she went out with a bang, if you'll pardon the expression." Skip looked down at the bed.

"Jesus!" Lou's voice kicked up a notch. "Don't you have a shred of decency?"

Skip just gave him a jaded curl of his lips and then continued with his explanation. "What I have, Lieutenant, is twelve hours of overtime, sore feet, change for coffee, and a plaque on a wall downtown that says I'm licensed to stand here and spout off at length." Skip enjoyed irritating

Lou. "On the other hand, what you have is a beautiful woman who ended a glorious night of lovemaking with a broken neck and a gunshot wound."

"What do you mean? Her neck was broken?" My heart jumped into my throat.

"So the cause of death wasn't the gunshot wound?" Lou asked.

"Well, that's what we're trying to determine. We discovered her broken neck when we started to move the body. My guess at this point is that they broke her neck, then shot her. But whoever killed her didn't do it in the bed. You guys got any leads? I understand they found some guy in bed with the corpse."

"The police have someone in mind." I went over to my side of the bed.

Lou listened while Skip gave him more details on their preliminary findings. I studied the bed, trying to put this in some sense of order, figure out what happened last night. But all I could think of was Carole. I fought not to remember the sound of her voice, her lips kissing me restlessly, and I shook my head to clear the fresh memory. I found it hard not to think of touching her in this same bed—where the police found her murdered. How the hell did somebody walk right in and kill her with me lying next to her? It burned me up to think of someone that good or that I was that stupid.

I looked down at the pillow I slept on and noticed a small discoloration on the white linen fabric, a yellowish stain. Barely noticeable, but definitely apparent once you inspected the fabric from a closer vantage point.

"Gitz, what are you doing?" Lou caught me kneeling before the pillow. "Remember what we said about tampering with evidence?"

Skip leaned over the bed. "Yeah, there's some kind of dried gunk on the pillow," he tapped at it with his pen. "It could be saliva. Already got a sample."

"Just checking for spiders, Lou." I said, peering under the bed.

"Oh, there's nothing under there now." Skip looked smug. "We found a box full of letters and pictures. I stuck it in the outer room with the other things forensics is dusting for prints."

"Why would someone break her neck and then shoot her?" I asked.

Skip threw up his hands and gave me a withering look. "Same reason they shot Kennedy? How the hell should I know? Maybe they wanted someone to think she was shot and killed. You guys are the detectives. You figure it out." He pulled at one of the forensic gloves, stretching the vinyl on his hand.

Lou crossed his arms in front of him. I knew it pissed him off to have me invite Skip to speculate on what might have happened, but Lou didn't really sound as if he believed in my innocence. I tried to digest everything Skip had told us about the murder. My mind must have just come back on-line because the obvious had suddenly become clear to me. Someone shot Carole to make it appear I had killed her.

I looked around the room. "What happened to the gun?"

"What the hell are you talking about, Gitz?" Lou stared at me, arms still crossed.

"Someone shot Carole to make it look like I killed her. So where's the gun? I wasn't carrying my gun when we came back here. I didn't even take it out of my desk. Send a couple of guys over to my office right now and you'll find it there, bottom right drawer of my desk."

Skip's eyes widened as he stared at me. I should've waited until Lou and I were alone.

"You mean the cops think you did it?" Skip stared from Lou to me and back.

"Who's to say she didn't own a gun?" Lou countered me, ignoring Skip.

"For Pete's sake, Lou, cut me some slack!" I snapped. Then another thought came to mind. "What about her neck? If I had already broken her neck, why would I shoot her? The gunshot would only draw attention to me."

"The cops think you did it? You're the suspect?" Skip repeated.

"But somebody heard something and called it in," Lou added.

"The cops think you did it?" Skip muttered a third time. His brain must have been stuck in neutral.

I nodded. "Yes, Skip. The police found me here this morning in bed with her. Got it?" I turned back to Lou. "C'mon, you can't deny this smells like a set-up."

"Gitz, they found you at the crime scene after it happened. And that's all the D.A. is gonna give a rat's ass about." His eyes softened a bit.

"Nelson can blow me."

"We'd better go now, Gitz. Skip, I expect a full report from the coroner's office to back up your theory." Lou pointed the almighty finger at him.

I tried to keep all the facts together in my head as we moved through the townhouse again. Aside from the fact they found me in bed with Carole, there didn't seem to be any solid evidence that I'd committed any crime. But there wasn't anything to prove my innocence, either. Beyond all the anguish I felt, the cop in me couldn't figure out how all this had happened. Even with a silencer, I'm sure I'd have heard the muffled shot or caught the stench of gunpowder in the air. How could someone have pulled it all off so well?

In the hallway, I noticed an open shoe-box full of letters, likely the one Skip mentioned. One of the other officers called Lou over to him. I glanced around to be certain no one paid any attention to me, and I took a peek inside. Photos, letters, and cards haphazardly thrown into the crammed box, except for one thick stack of letters all bound by a rubber band.

Checking both ends of the hallway again, I made sure everyone had something to keep their minds and eyes away from me. Using the hem of my shirt to keep from leaving my prints, I reached into the box and began flipping through the contents. I studied a frequent return address. Peering out from the slush of Get Well's and Happy Birthdays, one label caught my eye. The address was out of state, though I recognized the name immediately.

"Cappie," I whispered, snatching the letter.

As I grabbed it, I uncovered a picture of a woman sticking out of the corner of the box. Carole. Her earthy smile hit me hard. God, it hurt like a gut shot, too much to bear. I grabbed the shoebox and stuffed it under my coat with the letter. It wasn't the wisest move I'd made considering the circumstances, but I wanted to hold on to any part of her I could.

"Who the hell are you people?" a man's voice came from the entrance of the apartment.

"Just hold it right there, mister!" Lou whipped out his badge and shoved it in the face of our unexpected guest. "Just who the hell are you?"

"What the hell's going on here? Where's Carole?" The tall, well-dressed man startled the group like cockroaches caught in the light.

"Why don't we start with you answering our questions first?" Lou insisted. "What's your name? You got ID?"

He pulled out an expensive leather wallet and held out his driver's license for Lou.

"Derek Simmons," he said. "I'm Carole's fiancé."

FOUR

I was still numb from the shock of Carole's death and now this? A fiancé—Carole's fiancé—appears out of the blue? This was more than a body could take in one day, and mine didn't fare too well at all. My head hadn't stopped pounding. In fact, it had reached a jackhammer's pace.

Lou decided it would be better if he explained everything to Mr. Simmons without my being there to confuse things. I agreed, though I had a few questions I would have liked to ask Derek myself. Oddly, I didn't have the strength or desire to argue. But I had more important questions to ponder, like why hadn't Carole said anything to me about her fiancé? How did she manage to keep him a secret? And how did she keep us a secret from him? Too bad I couldn't ask her now. It hurt too much to even think about it.

My head was hot, and I felt a rush like a fever sweeping over my face. Nausea suddenly hit like a baseball bat to the gut. I hurried toward the door and outside. Lou appeared behind me as I vomited into a shrub. What the hell was wrong with me? I straightened up long enough to hear him tell an officer to take me home as soon as I was able. I pulled my coat tighter to keep the shoebox hidden, then bent back over the bush and puked again. Ten minutes later, I stretched out on the back seat of a cruiser. The box dug into my side beneath my coat. As another wave of nausea hit, I prayed I could hold it together until I got home.

The officer drove around to the back of Deacon's, cutting from the main drag to an alley running the length of the Short North. We pulled up next to Deacon's Saab, splashing it via the pothole he had promised he'd have filled a year ago. Served his penny-pinching ass right.

Officer Reynolds met my eyes in his rearview mirror. "Due respect, Lou's neck is on the line letting you go home. Best stay here and leave this up to the department, sir."

I nodded and pulled myself out of the car. I kept the shoebox pressed tightly against me until he was out of sight. There were two freight elevators next to the loading dock. One of the elevators led directly to my place, quick and easy for those not up to the challenge, but most of my clients used the front stairwell. You wouldn't know to look at the elevators that they still worked. They appeared too old and neglected to do anything. A dirty orange rust covered the once shiny steel frame. I stepped in and turned my elevator key, trying to put the day out of my mind. As the elevator clanked up, I absently touched the rust with my fingertips and it flaked away. I'd spent an afternoon once trying to scrape off the rust and decay from it with no appreciable effect. And like John, who had tried before me, I simply gave up.

It felt good to be home again. The huge, three-room loft served as both workspace and refuge, which is what made it so attractive to me in the first place. Everything nice and handy, well within reach and no long drive when I'd put in some overtime on the job. I handled most of my cases in the outer area, where I had arranged a simple set-up; a desk, two chairs, two steel cabinets for case files, and a coffeemaker. It provided a superb view of a painted mural on the building across the parking lot. In the larger second room, I kept a stationary bike, a queen-sized brass bed, tv, sofa, and a baby grand piano. A book rack filled with sheet music of all my favorite songs and vinyls of my favorite artists sat between the piano and my stereo. I prefer my music to be tangible, not some downloaded file. Same as my case files—just paper and my handwriting, which almost no one but me can read.

Up here, amidst Coltrane and Calloway, Sting and Sanborn, I tried to forget about the world, and occasionally wrote a little music of my own. It would take years for me to be as good as Dr. John or George Duke. My delusions of grandeur took me as far as my front door and no farther than the fire escape. Music relieved my tensions, picked me up when my mood was sour. It was like a good friend who didn't ask me a lot of questions. My own form of therapy.

Lately, I'd been avoiding anything to do with my ex-wife. She seemed to make problems out of every little thing, and I didn't want to travel that road anymore. Not only had she gone out of her way to make my life a living hell lately, but she also took special joy in telling me she was dating some new "mature guy who offered her stability"—an insurance salesman. Code for wuss, no doubt.

I dropped the crushed shoebox on the table next to my phone. I ignored my voicemail notifications. I desperately needed a shower and clean clothes. I put on a little soft music, Angela Bofill's "I Try". I loved her stuff. She had a voice that could make you forget your mother's name—smoother than a twelve-year-old scotch and softer than mink. A bluesy torch song always made me feel good. I needed to feel good about something now, even if only for a little while. Three songs later, I stretched out on the sofa. The shower had relaxed me more than I thought it would. The record player had long since stopped by the time I awoke from my nap.

The clock chimed nine and the noise from downstairs drifted up like steam from a sauna. I threw on some slacks and a sweatshirt and headed down the front stairs to see what was cooking in the bar. The smells that met me in the stairwell reminded me of something particularly important. Deacon's served a pretty decent club sandwich with fries.

As usual, the place was packed. People were shoulder-to-shoulder, like bees in a honeycomb. Folks were drinking and dancing away their miseries with their money stretched out just ahead of them. A jazz trio rocked the stage tonight. Redhaired Rita stood off in a corner, offering advice to a co-worker, perhaps on connecting with one of her past lives. John counted the customers watching the band. Business always came first with John.

"Excuse me, you're standing in my way," a breathy woman's voice called from behind me. I hadn't realized that I had walked right in front of the bar and in direct view of the band.

I turned and found myself stunned. Her long auburn hair swept to one side over her shoulder. She wore a black dress that clung to her like a python and left little to the imagination. Her smooth, well-defined jawline had a slight hint of a cleft. I guessed her to be in her late twenties and looking for the kind of trouble I wasn't interested in.

"I'm sorry," I shifted to her right. "Is this seat taken?" I inquired about the barstool.

She looked at me like I'd just run over her dog or something. Then she drew the gold handbag she carried close to her, pulling one leg across the other.

"I was waiting for someone but go ahead." Her voice showed reluctance.

"Appreciate it." I slid in and signaled for a beer. "Listen, if your friend shows up, I'd be glad to move," I said.

"That's one I haven't heard." She arched an eyebrow. "Maybe a bit too rehearsed."

"It wasn't a line," I said. Deacon set a beer in front of me and I took a big swig.

"If it wasn't a line, what do you call it?" A smirk curled out of the corner of her mouth. "Don't pretend you're actually trying to have an intelligent conversation."

Now she had pissed me off. "Look, let's cut to the chase here." I looked straight at her, glaring. "Why don't you just tell me to fuck off now and save us both some time? I promise you I'm only interested in the seat." I clenched my teeth together to keep from getting any more irritated with her.

A slack jawed look suddenly washed over her face. She appeared dumbfounded, speechless, and caught off guard. She straightened in her chair and looked at me quizzically. I drank my beer. So what if I seemed harsh? I didn't really care that I'd struck a nerve. I just hated when some women assumed every man's single interest was to slam them against the headboard.

"Look, I'm a little cautious, all right?" Her voice softened. "That doesn't make me a bitch."

"You don't owe me an explanation, lady." I finished my beer and ordered another.

"The name's McCrae. Jordan Taylor McCrae." She turned to me with the smile of a Cheshire cat and teeth just as bright. "I guess I thought you were some creep." She seemed sincere enough, but the sincere part of me had already left the building.

"Well, it's been nice talking with you, but I think I see some friends my own age over there." I put more ice in my voice than I should have. But she had come out first with claws bared. It had been a horrific day, and I let my mouth run the show.

It's not that I was mad at this one woman in particular. I was just mad. My rage had wormed its way out through the first open vent available—my big mouth. Maybe I should've allowed myself more time alone in my loft. Or maybe, with everything that had happened in the last twenty-four hours, I was trying hard not to feel anything. I wanted to be numb. What bothered me most was that I felt more than a little afraid of what I'd feel if I let myself feel anything. I got up and paid for two beers.

"Hey, I didn't deserve that!" Jordan called out to me.

"Right, I'm sorry. I guess we both made a mistake, didn't we? Have a good evening." I took my beer and left her.

I made my way towards the back of the bar. I didn't want to be mean to her; that's not my usual style, though I was sure the events of the day had influenced my demeanor. I understood where Jordan was coming from. Some assholes don't know how to take no for an answer and they go from compliments to confrontation when they don't get what they want. A woman's need to be guarded could mean the difference between life and death, and most guys just don't think about that. Unfortunately, my bad day just reinforced that sad fact for Jordan. At the core of my anger was knowing Carole should've had her guard up the night she died, but she thought she was safe with me. She probably believed nothing could happen to her, lying in my arms, warm and protected. Suddenly, I didn't feel very manly at all.

I needed to be alone, away from the crowd and the crap. I staggered back up to my place in under a minute, still toting my beer, running from the noise of the bar and the sound of my own thoughts. But my thoughts didn't stop hounding me when I shut my door. My mind replayed the image of Carole's eyes, cold and drained of their light, like a lurid vision that stained the mirror of my soul. Deep down, I felt I was to blame. It felt as though I were coming apart at the seams as I struggled against the grief and rage. But now wasn't the time to give in to my feelings. Someone had committed a vicious crime, and no one wanted justice more than me.

At times like this, I didn't need a reassuring voice with advice on handling things. I needed the sound of my piano, the feel of ivory against my fingertips, to keep things in perspective. I needed the music to help make clear what had happened last night. Carole would have understood the necessity of me keeping my feelings in check. She knew solitude often did more good than talking things out. I sat down at the piano.

"You and I need to talk, old buddy." Deacon slid in without my noticing. The sight of him rattled me for a second. I hadn't even heard the door. Damn, had this happened at Carole's last night?

"Been a long day, Deac. What's going on?" I stroked the keys lightly.

"Rita's tending bar. Thought you might want some company, at least some company you could stomach right now." He had obviously heard about Carole. "How 'bout we go for a walk or something?"

"No thanks." I continued to play, avoiding eye contact with him. "Got a lot on my mind."

He sat down on the piano bench next to me. "Sorry to hear about Carole. She seemed like good people."

I paused slightly. "How'd you get wind of it?"

"Skip dropped by just before you came down," he explained.

"He still trying to get his band booked?"

"You really want to talk about Skip?"

I glanced up to see him staring at my bottle of beer rather strange-ly. I noticed he held a bottle of Jack Daniels and two glasses. I really didn't want to smile, but here was John being John; the kind of guy you couldn't say no to, not often anyway.

"What happened?" he asked and handed me the bottle.

"I wish I knew." I poured myself a healthy shot of whiskey and then one for John. "Someone got into her apartment and killed her—with me lying right next to her."

"What kind of sick bastard would do a thing like that?"

I shook my head in silence as I stared into my glass. "Actually, the cops think I'm the sick bastard."

A look of shock spread across his wide face and then receded into anger. "Bullshit," he said.

I tilted my head back to empty my glass. "They found me there with the body. It doesn't look as though they'll need to prove motive. They know as much as I do at this point."

John leaned over and filled my glass. "They'll find out who did it, Gitz, they will."

"Skip said the son of a bitch broke her neck, then shot her. Whoever killed her didn't care about me or I'd be dead along with Carole. It's deliberate. I know I'm being set up, but of course, the cops think I'm as guilty as sin."

"Even Lou?" He gave me a discerning look.

"I'm not sure Lou knows what to think. He knows I wouldn't just kill somebody. I think he's more worried than I am." I chased the whiskey with a shot of beer.

"Maybe you need to give Mel a call, get some legal advice," John suggested.

"An attorney isn't going to help me with my real problem here, Deac."

"Which is what?"

"Finding out who killed Carole and doing to them what they did to her." I finished my whiskey and put the glass on the floor.

John sighed. "You and I both know where thinking like that is going to get you, Gitz."

"Then what? I should let the police handle this and stay out of the way?"

I didn't want to get mad at John, he wasn't the enemy. The person who killed Carole deserved to feel the pain of my rage. But that didn't mean that I would let anyone tell me I shouldn't be involved. That decision was made for me the moment Carole died.

I sighed, wearily. "It isn't just catching the killer, Deac, it's the fact that somehow I let it happen. I was there. I was lying right next to her. I don't even know if she called to me."

I closed the piano, bent to pick up my glass, and turned toward the fire escape. I couldn't afford to break down now. I wouldn't allow myself the luxury of wallowing in my grief, not before I knew the name of Carole's killer.

"Eddie, wait...I—"

"—S'okay. I'm fine."

"Do you think it was somebody out to get you? Maybe an old case?"

"Maybe, but then why not just kill me? Why her?" I spun around to face him again.

"Maybe someone had it in for Carole, and you just happened to be there."

"I'm not ready to buy that either," I said. "Last night, I thought I knew everything I needed to know about this woman. Why didn't she tell me if someone was out to get her?"

He shrugged, refilling my glass. "I dunno. She must've had a reason. Maybe she was trying to protect you. Maybe she didn't want whoever was after her coming after you as well."

"Maybe it was Derek Simmons."

He stared at me. "Who the hell is Derek Simmons?"

"He showed up at the crime scene earlier, claiming to be Carole's fiancé."

"Fiancé? Where the hell did he come from?" John set his glass down.

I suddenly remembered what she said when we first went into her bedroom, how we had never spent the night together there. Maybe the fiancé was the reason we never spent the night at her place before last night. But how had she hidden him so well? He obviously didn't live with her. No telltale signs. No sports mags lying around. No razors. No dirty socks. No mess. It looked all too feminine.

"I'd never seen him before, and Carole never mentioned ever dating anyone else, let alone being engaged." I sipped the whiskey slowly.

"If she was engaged, why did she date you in the first place?" He helped himself to another drink. "No offense pal, but he could have walked in on the two of you at any time and made the situation very nasty. Why would she risk it?"

I didn't answer him.

"Don't take this the wrong way, Gitz. But maybe you didn't know the girl as well as you thought. Something doesn't figure right if you say she's got a fiancé and never told you about it. Some women are devious like that, you don't know," he said.

God, I wish she were here to tell me. "Look, Deac, I think I need to be by myself for a while, okay?"

"Sure buddy, no problem." He hoisted himself from the bench and headed for the door. "I'll get with you tomorrow."

"John, thanks."

I sat there and listened for the door to close behind him, thinking painfully about what he'd said about Carole. Did she hide her fiancé from me, or could this Derek Simmons be a fake? And why had he only now shown up? Trying to make sense of it all only made the throbbing in my head worse. Fortunately, John had left the bottle of whiskey.

With drink in hand, I stretched out on the sofa and made one more attempt to sort out this nightmare. I wished this was nothing more than a bad dream. But I had more questions than I had answers.

If Carole and Derek were engaged and the relationship went sour, why not come out and say so? Was there a reason she didn't want me to know about him? Given that they had a relationship, having him admit it out in the open would only implicate him if their parting was bitter. I thought for a moment about what I knew, which didn't amount to much. I held up the bottle of Jack and stared across the room through the dark-colored liquid. Had I been looking at this from some hazy shade of pain, or was there more going on than I realized?

FIVE

My head still throbbed when I got up the next morning around 9:20. It was Tuesday. The headaches and the nausea I'd had for the last few days weren't going away quietly and that bugged me. Normally, I'd start the day with a thirty-minute ride on my bike, crank out about sixty sit-ups, and finish with some dumbbell curls and two or three sets on the bench press. Didn't matter if I'd found the bottom of a bottle the night before.

Instead I crawled into the shower and stood under the water until it turned ice cold, and then I peeled off my soaking wet clothes and draped them over the shower curtain rod. I dried off and threw on a pair of black jeans and a blue T-shirt. Even after a night like I'd just had, breakfast was still a priority. I made a strong pot of coffee and sliced up some fresh grapefruit and melon to ease my hunger and kill the taste of the booze.

I followed a simple day-to-day routine when working on a case, keeping track of places I had to visit in and out of the city, people I'd have to see. I also kept a log of where I'd planned to go in case something ever went wrong and I needed to be found. I always left word with John about my plans. He knew how to track me down if it was necessary.

My list for today was simple:

1. GET BACK INTO CAROLE'S APARTMENT.

2. SEE WHAT I COULD DIG UP AT THE CREDIT BUREAU.

3. FIND OUT MORE ABOUT DEREK SIMMONS.

4. FIND OUT WHERE CAROLE'S OFFICE WAS LOCATED.

5. GET IN TOUCH WITH CAPPIE.

The last item was more personal than business. I felt I at least owed Carole the decency of letting her relatives know what had happened to her. Even if Cappie had already been told, my conscience would rest a little easier knowing I made the attempt. It wouldn't be easy, though. How do you tell a man his granddaughter has died? Especially someone I had a personal, intimate connection with.

I made my way to my office and grabbed a notebook to jot down any interesting bits of information I might come across. Good organizational skills were necessary for any private investigator worth their salt. Given that I was also looking for a killer, taking my gun along didn't seem like a bad idea either.

The Baretta 92FS had long been my weapon of choice; sleek, Trijicon night-sights, staggered clip, Parkerized black finish, and just the right size for my large hands. I packed my gun and two spare clips into my shoulder holster and fitted them both around my back, securing it just beneath my shoulder blade.

It was 11:15 am when I pulled up to Carole's complex. The off-beat rumbling of my Camaro's engine reminded me that I'd need a tune-up sometime soon. I shut off the engine and coasted in front of her town-house, still sealed with yellow crime scene tape. The scarce number of cars assured me most of the other residents were off to work or wherever, making my chances good for getting inside the place again. This appealed to my devious side; the mischievous scamp who loved sneaking into forbidden places. Still, I hated to take anything or anyone for granted. The last thing I needed was some Rambo-granny sneaking up on me with a broom.

I could hear the sound of music and clapping from a half-opened door as I got out of my car. The neighbor in 2286 seemed to be partying a wee bit early in the day, I thought. Curious to see what the ruckus was about, I followed the sound and put away my small packet of tools, stuffing them back into my pocket. I didn't want to take the chance of anyone questioning why I wanted to get into Carole's place. I stopped and listened to what sounded like a cadence call and then knocked. No answer. I thumped louder and suddenly the sound ceased. I could hear someone moving toward the door and then a face peered at me through the cracked door.

A woman answered, breathing heavily with a terrycloth towel pressed against the side of her face. She wore a tight, Day-Glo yellow body suit and white tennis shoes. She didn't seem much older than I, late-thirties or so. Her bright, orange-colored hair was pulled back into a ponytail and she wore a matching headband over her brow. She had a slightly plump figure, but nothing that would turn a man off. She didn't seem too pleased that I had interrupted her morning routine.

"Can I help you?" she puffed. "I don't need anything."

"I'm not here to sell anything." I reached into my pocket and handed her my card.

She snatched it quickly and then closed the screen door between us. As she scanned it, her eyes lit up. "Are you with the police?"

I shook my head. "No, I'm a private investigator."

"Oh, a private detective." She straightened and stuck her chest out, stretching her upper back. "What brings you to my door?"

"I'd like to ask you a few questions about your next-door neighbor if that's alright." I kept my eyes locked on hers. "If now is a good time."

She studied me, lazily, moving her eyes back and forth between me and the card I gave her. "No, no, now is just fine." She stepped back and allowed me into her apartment. "Please come in, I was just finishing up anyway." She scurried across the room to shut off her phone's playlist, buffing her face again with the towel. "Just give me a moment."

She bounced across the room the way some young girls do when they get an unexpected visit from the captain of the football team. I never played football, but I had at least gotten her to take me at my word so far. I stood next to a wicker table near the door, noticing all the exercise equipment that dominated the place. There was a treadmill, a sit-up bench, a bench press, all squeezed into the living room. I spied a Smith Machine sitting awkwardly on the deck outside. I'd have laid odds that she watched every workout video ever made. And I thought I was a health nut.

After about a minute or two, she finally came back and spoke to me again. "My name is Joan, Joan Richards." She cleared a spot for us both on the sofa. "How can I help you Mr. Gideon?"

"I'm investigating the murder of the woman who lived next door. Did you know her?" I asked.

"Carole? Oh, well not really. I mean I knew her, but it was just kind of a casual thing." She shifted into something of a dramatic pose. "We spoke to one another and I picked up her mail whenever she was out of town, but she really hadn't lived here long enough for me to really get to know her. Do you carry a gun?" There was a look in her eyes I wasn't sure I should acknowledge just at that moment, something catty.

"Uh, yes. Did she have many friends, people who stopped by on a regular basis?"

She brought her hand to her mouth and let it glide down the length of her neck to her breast. I struggled to keep my eyes on her eyes. "No one that I recollect. There was no steady man around if that's what you mean. I'm an R.N. and I work in the evenings. By the time I get home, I'm too wiped out to notice anyone who might have stayed the night. I pulled a double the night she was killed, so I didn't even hear about it until later that evening. Y'know, you have very striking shoulders. Do you work out often?"

I ignored the question. "Do you know where she worked?"

She wet her lips with her tongue, sliding it from one end of her mouth to the other as she thought for a moment. I tried to keep from blushing, not sure if I'd misread her signals. I brought my hand over my mouth and pretended to yawn.

"I saw her on my way home one day, turning into one of those new office complexes on Shrock Road." Again she stroked her neckline. "Like I said, it was just kind of a casual thing."

"Did she ever mention anything to you about someone giving her a hard time, an old boyfriend or something?"

She sighed. "If anything, Carole and I had one thing in common. We kept to ourselves. I didn't involve myself with her personal life and she kindly did the same. So there really isn't a whole lot I can tell you about that."

This felt like a dead end, and it was time to move on.

"If you think of anything else that might help, just call my office." I pointed to the card again.

"Is this your home number or office line? In case I should think of something after normal business hours, of course."

I made a beeline for the door. I swear I could feel her steamy breath on my back the whole time as I was leaving. I jumped in my car and waved kindly as she delivered her most delicious parting smile. I'd have to try to get into Carole's place some other time. Besides, my headache and nausea had become unbearable and I had to see a doctor.

SIX

Despite culling very little new information from her neighbor Joan, my visit to Carole's complex gave me a place to start working for answers. It came at a very a painful price. I should have known better than to think that I could just go back there without it affecting me in some way. A part of me half expected Carole to be standing at her door, hair undone, rushing off to work with no more than time enough for a glancing kiss and a wave goodbye.

I headed east across town for Dr. Kamen's office, hoping to get something for whatever was twisting my insides. The doctor's office was a small clinic just off the freeway exit at Interstate 71 and Morse Road. Nick Kamen had been the family doctor since before Stephie was born. Knowing me as well as he did—I make my annual checkup, but I don't come in for every sniffle or minor ache—he had his MA usher me quickly into one of those dull-painted rooms. She took the standard assessment-weight, blood pressure, and temperature. I described my symptoms to her, and then when he entered a moment later, repeated my symptoms without the details of everything else I'd gone through. He took a blood sample to run a few tests, then gave me some pills to ease the nausea with instruction: *Take with food.*

I walked over to the strip mall across the street looking for a quick bite and something cool and cheap to wash down the pills. Instead I found myself stumbling into a jewelry store, McKay's Diamond and Gold, the third largest jeweler in the city, almost exclusively advertised by word-of-mouth. Whether I meant to go in or not is still a mystery.

"Can I help you sir?" An older gentleman greeted me. His kind, plain face matched his grey suit. His posture was enviable, good, and straight the way his mother probably reminded him to stand. He looked to be in his late fifties, just a wisp of grey along the temples. The puffy dollops under his eyes formed half-moon shapes as he smiled.

"Is there anything in particular you're looking for?"

"No... I came in the wrong door." I said.

"Trying to make sure she doesn't see us, right?" he smiled.

"I beg your pardon?"

He moved back behind a glass case, glancing up and down as if to draw my attention to the sparkling baubles beneath his hand. I wondered if maybe he'd been working too hard. "I've seen that look you've got a number of times, young man. You've got a special young lady in mind and you're thinking about her quite a bit these days."

"Okay." I went along with him.

"Not to worry, son. We've still got that special gift you selected for her in the back." He pointed down into the glass case. "See, we've even left the sold sticker in its place."

I didn't have a clue as to what he was talking about. I wondered if maybe he thought I was someone else when I suddenly realized I'd been here before.

"It's Mr. Gideon, isn't it?"

I nodded without a word. The special gift he referred to was a gold butterfly pendant I'd planned to give to Carole as a surprise. In all the confusion of the last few days, I had all but forgotten I'd paid him a deposit of three hundred dollars and promised to pick up the butterfly later this month.

"Give me just a moment and I'll get the item for you." He hurried off before I could speak.

I stood there staring down into the glass case, the memory of my last visit now clear in my mind. The glare from the jewels nearly blinded me. My eyes widened at the diamonds and emeralds, pearls, and sapphires. The last time I bought a ring I could barely make the payments on the one-eighth carat I gave Cassandra. I didn't make much more money now and the price of a decent ring could put more than a dent in my financial picture. I remember dreaming of what might be nice to slide upon Carole's finger and watch as her jaw would drop to the ground. God, where was my head?

The salesman returned carrying a small black box. He gingerly lifted the butterfly from the case and held it out to me, like a newborn babe emerging from the womb. He slowly moved his fingers beneath it, animating the wings as though it were alive. Staring down at it, I almost believed it was real. I wanted to believe it was real.

"I'm sure your lady friend will love this, Mr. Gideon." He grinned. I wagered he'd done this a million times—reeling unsuspecting buyers in with a Bassmaster's ease, waiting for them to try and pull back against the line, letting them exhaust every excuse they could muster before yanking them up to where he wanted.

"Actually something has come up," I weakly offered. "Now isn't such a good time."

"Well, if you're thinking about affordability, I might be able to help." He coaxed. "We have several payment plans available. I'm sure one of them would work well within your budget."

I wanted to laugh. My budget consisted of whatever was left after paying my rent and what my ex-wife might have been kind enough to leave me after getting her share. The child support I didn't mind, but she made more than I did last year and she still claims it's not enough.

"What's her name, son?" he asked.

"I'm sorry?" The pin still held me with its glitter.

"Your lady friend. What's her name?"

"Carole. Her name's Carole," I said.

"She must be very special to you."

I nodded in silence.

"I lost my special someone a long time ago. She went away rather suddenly. We spent so many wonderful years together." His eyes softened, "Nowadays people just come and go in each other's lives, never taking the time to appreciate what they have."

I found myself feeling strange, as though his loneliness had suddenly become a part of me. In his eyes I saw a glimmer of what love had shown him, the beauty, the wonder, the loss. His words hit me right between the eyes and twisted their way into my heart. I knew what it felt like to still love someone who had gone. As I stared into his eyes, I realized he had let me look into his heart, and there I found a hole, a piece of his soul missing. That part of himself he'd given to the woman he loved.

"If you really care for this woman young man, tell her," his voice cracked. "Tell her every chance you get. Never let a moment slip by that you don't."

I didn't have the heart to tell him the truth. I made up some lie about not being able to get in touch with her like I wanted and told him I'd be back in a week or so. He merely gave me a cheerful smile and a wave as I left. I opened the bottle of medicine and took two pills. The caplets were coated and I figured to hell with eating right now.

SEVEN

I left the Columbus Credit Bureau at about two-thirty. The hot sun and the humidity made the day near unbearable. The gun in my shoulder holster moved back and forth against my back like a giant slug from all the sweat. I stripped the gun off and threw it in the glove box. I peeled the second skin my shirt had become to let a cool breeze dry us both. I went to the trunk where I kept a spare T-shirt and pulled it over my head, then grabbed a light jacket from the backseat. Keeping an extra set of clothing in the car had become an occupational prerequisite.

My car had been parked in the direction of the sun and considering the length of time I spent at the CCB tracking down where Carole worked, my vinyl seats had reached the perfect temperature for frying. I draped the jacket over the seat to keep my neck and arms from touching the seat. I'd found out through Gerri, my contact in Records, that Carole worked for Prentiss Securities. Just as Joan had said, they were located just off of Shrock Road. Prentiss had only been in business for the last eight years. But in that time they had made a killing.

Prentiss specialized in new issues, small companies that started out as back of the car or basement operations. Their tech savvy and aggressive marketing turned many a venture into a solid business. Most of the execs earned upper six-figure-salaries, more than I'd see in my line of work.

I had Gerri also run a check on Derek Simmons' to find his place of employment. Imagine my surprise when I learned that Derek also worked for Prentiss. The rumbling in my stomach did the Can-Can at this bit of news.

***

Prentiss Securities occupied one of many buildings within the mega-office complex. The builders had designed the area like a new development for homes; winding drives, pristine landscaping to give the allure of affluence, breathtaking panoramic views of steel and stone jutting up from the ground as though God Himself demanded their creation.

I came upon a charming young lady in the lobby of the Prentiss building. Kelly, as her name badge read, was smartly dressed in a grey jacket and apple red blouse. Her coal black hair was cut short and even to her jawline. I studied her with wonder as she, like most well-trained receptionists, handled a barrage of incoming calls with eloquence and efficiency. She had the look of an Ivory Soap girl, clean, flawless skin and a demeanor of wholesome goodness, 99.9 percent pure.

"Welcome to Prentiss Securities, can I help you?" She looked up from the phones long enough to acknowledge me.

"I hope so." I dug into my pockets for my card. "My name is Eddie Gideon, I'm a private investigator. I was wondering if I could ask a few questions about Carole Spenser."

The sparkle in Kelly's eyes retreated and the warmth of her red-lipped smile withered at my request. She took off her headset, laid it to one side and slid from behind her desk. She brought her hands to her face briefly, dabbed her fingers against the corners of her eyes. I was touched that someone else cared, really cared about Carole.

She forced a smile again. "I'm sorry, I don't know why I did that." She reached in her desk drawer for a tissue. "Carole and I weren't close, but she was always nice to me. I'll miss that."

For all of a brief second, I felt the rumbling within me shift, taking on a more agitated tone, more piercing. I focused my eyes on Kelly. She knew a part of Carole I had been distanced from, though I knew well of Carole's tenderness and compassion. I too had been touched by the magic of her smile. Already I began to count the things I'd miss about her.

"I apologize if I upset you. Carole was a friend of mine." I felt compelled to tell her.

A glint of her former radiance returned to her face.

"You're not with the police?"

"I'm kind of helping them with their investigation." Which was kind of true. "Can you tell me a little bit about what she did here? Maybe something that might help us figure out why she was killed?"

"I'll tell you what I know." She began softly. "Carole was a high-level trader, commodities and things like that. She didn't know it, but there was talk of making her a partner."

"A partner? That's interesting, considering she hadn't been here for very long." I added.

"Just in this office. Carole transferred here from one of our regional offices in Chicago. Because of her work there, she got the offer to come and work here at corporate headquarters. Mr. Prentiss himself walked her right through the door. She had so much to look forward to." She looked away from me.

"Can you think of anyone here who didn't get along with Carole?" I watched for any tell-tale gesture. "Did she have any enemies?"

Kelly giggled and shook her head. "I've learned you can't work in this business and not make any enemies. I'm sure there were a number of traders who didn't care for her, but they all respected her drive and business sense. Most nights she'd still be at it long after everyone had gone home. Sometimes she'd even get to the office before I did. I'd take her coffee all the time."

"So she never fought openly with anyone on the job?" I asked.

Kelly slid down into her chair and hunched up her shoulders as she leaned on her elbows. "Now that's a different story. There was one trader she used to get into it with quite a bit. She even slapped him once."

I decided to take a shot. "His name wouldn't happen to be Derek Simmons, would it?"

"You know him?" Her jaw dropped like a roller coaster.

"I thought he and Carole were engaged or something?"

She laughed aloud. "God, that lie again. Some of the other girls used to joke with Carole that she and Derek only fought so much to keep people from knowing they were getting married. Derek transferred from Chicago too. I guess they dated a few times, but I never knew of anything serious."

"Did you and Carole ever talk about anyone else she might have been seeing?"

"No, not really." she sighed. "I remember her telling me something about a guy she met in a bar once. She thought he was really nice, but that's about it."

I tried not to let Kelly see the look of disappointment making its way across my face. Maybe Carole wanted our relationship to be a secret too. Kelly's eyes suddenly moved behind me. She quickly put her headset back on and adjusted herself in her chair, doing her best to appear as I had found her when I first walked in. What the hell was this?

"Any messages for me, Kelly?" a voice drew closer.

"No sir, Mr. Simmons." She slowly raised her eyes to me again.

I turned. Derek and I now stood face to face. He had the look of a man who had his hands in money all the time. He was tall, slender, and smelled of something I probably couldn't afford. He wore a dark blue pin-striped suit with a white button-down oxford. Everything from his jeweled tie-clip to his gold collar bar screamed privileged and pampered. His slicked back hair stayed neatly tucked behind his tiny ears. His sea blue eyes focused tightly upon me as I extended my hand to him.

"Hello Mr. Simmons, I'm Eddie Gideon."

"I know who you are, you son-of-a-bitch!" he snapped.

Without another word he swung at me. As far as I knew, Derek didn't know anything about me being involved with the murder. I had hoped to find a way to get Derek to tell me a few things about his relationship with Carole. Maybe buy him a cup of coffee and find out how long he and I had been sharing the same woman. But that was before he put his fist in my face. We wrestled about on the floor of the lobby for a couple of minutes until the security guards burst in to escort me out of the building. One of them decided to take a cheap shot while my back was turned. I returned the favor with a roundhouse kick to his jaw before I stumbled off.

Damn Simmons, the little shit threw a mean left hook. I don't think I landed one punch. Derek yelled as I left that he knew what I'd done and I'd pay for it. I still didn't have a clue as to how he knew me. Kelly looked near tears again as she went about putting her desk back together. She didn't know what to make of all this and quite frankly, neither did I.

EIGHT

I arrived at the Franklin County Courthouse building at four-thirty, still nursing my sore jaw, and still pissed that Derek had caught me off guard. I'd probably have to see a dentist to make sure all of my fillings were still intact. It would serve Derek's butt right if I had my dentist fax his office a copy of my bill. Though in my present mood, I'd gladly pay my dentist double his fee for another round with Mr. Simmons.

It had been a while since I last heard from Lou and I wondered what he had come up with on the case. On occasion, Lou suffered from selective memory; an evasive tactic that often manifested itself in the form of acute forgetfulness. Lou often suffered from this ailment whenever someone had questions to ask, someone like me. I put in a call to police headquarters and learned Lou had left for a meeting with someone from the D.A.'s office, so I figured I'd catch him there.

The Courthouse occupied a site at the far south end of the downtown stretch. The building, made of smoked glass and marble, stretched twenty-six stories above the city. White stone pillars with a smooth finish and the open-air hallways, gave something of a Greco-Roman appearance to the place. With the number of people that moved in and about, one might think this was a pretty friendly place, unless you had a reason for being here. Police officers, traffic violators, first-timers, repeat offenders and attorneys bustled through these halls, waiting for their chance to face one another in the chambers of some judge.

I crossed the lobby and for some reason, felt a twinge as I headed for the elevators. It took me a moment to realize that someone was calling my name. I didn't recognize the voice at first until I heard a woman call out.

"Goddammit, Eddie, stop!"

I'd heard that phrase once too often not to know it was Cassandra.

Cassandra Gideon, my former bride, still made my heart jump every time I looked into those grey eyes. And she was just as beautiful and as angry as the day she divorced me. She stood a solid five-foot-seven inches with lengthy chestnut brown hair that whipped across her shoulders as she stormed toward me. The look she gave me was also remarkably familiar, reminding me of many heated moments between us. I wasn't sure what I had done to rile her this time, but it didn't look like she wanted to talk nicely. Damn, why did I have to run into her now?

She smacked me with her purse. "You asshole, how could you do that to Stephie? She was counting on you!"

"What?" I held up my arms to defend myself. "What did I do?"

"Where the hell were you last night?!" she hissed.

It came back to me like a bad bowl of chili. I was supposed to take Stephie out to dinner. She'd planned this father-daughter get together for months, picking out the restaurant, a dress and everything. And like a jackass, I blew it.

"Cassandra, I'm sorry I—"

"—I don't give a damn about your excuses Eddie," she cut me off. "You made a promise and fucked up! You left me to deal with the mess you made. What the hell could you have been thinking, Eddie?"

"If you give me a chance to explain, Sands, I can—"

"—Don't you even care about your daughter? She stood there half the night waiting for you. She called, and every time it went straight to voicemail. She waited for her father to tell her how beautiful she looked." Her eyes became watery. "I thought if nothing else, your daughter still meant something to you. I guess you just don't give a damn about us. God, I hate you."

Funny how after all this time, whenever Cassandra told me she hated me, it still cut into me like a jagged knife. No matter how many times I heard it, the words always shook me the way it did that first time. But knowing I'd broken my daughter's heart was far worse, and given the last two days, my own self-esteem hit an all-time low. Leaving Stephie was one of many deep regrets from my divorce. But even though it tore me apart, I knew leaving her with Cassandra was for the best in the long run.

I sighed. "You're right, I'm an asshole."

She huffed. "So what was it, Eddie? Did somebody die or what?"

I was ill-prepared to get into this again, especially with Cassandra. I didn't feel comfortable talking about my lover with my ex-wife and she'd definitely struck a nerve. Rather than give her the condensed version of the last few days, I merely shook my head and turned away.

"Eddie?"

"Not now, Sands," I said without looking back.

But Cassandra wasn't about to leave it at that. She rushed up beside me, clutching at my arm. "Hey, what the hell's going on with you, are you in some kind of trouble?"

"I'm always in trouble, remember?" I tried to smile.

"Don't screw with me Eddie Gideon. I can tell just by looking at you something's not right. C'mon dammit, talk to me."

A charge shot through my hand as she reached out to me, a warmth that reminded me of a time when Cassandra and I shared more than a crummy two-bedroom apartment with no heat and lousy plumbing. In our brief six years as husband and wife, there was little we didn't openly give to one another.

But pain was something I never quite knew how to relate in words. And if the words existed that could describe the depth of what I felt, I didn't know where to find them. Like most boys, I learned as I grew up that a man bears his pain in silence. I had been a man since the age of five. I never cried when my mother died, never uttered a word when they lowered her body quietly into the ground. As much as I may have wanted to share this pain, my pain with Cassandra, the truth was I simply didn't know how.

"You never told me why you're here." I changed the subject.

She began to fidget. "I... uh, I had to check on some paperwork. Robert has asked me to marry him."

I stood there dazed, waiting for Cassandra to correct what I'd just heard. Did she say marry?

"Excuse me?" I stammered.

She shifted back and forth. "I had planned to tell you last night, but you never showed. I wanted you to talk to Stephie about it."

"Why? Haven't you told her?'

"Yes, but she's been very resistant to Rob's attempts at building a bond."

I laughed abruptly. "Building a bond?"

"Robert is trying to become a father figure to her, a decent role model." Her voice had become almost a shout. "I would think you'd want to encourage her."

Now I was pissed. "You want me to encourage my kid to call some other guy, Daddy? Have you lost your damn mind? You tell Rob to shove it up his ass. Stephie's got a father!"

"She needs more than an occasional visit whenever you have the time, Eddie." She snapped back. "Robert is a good man and he really cares about Stephie, and dammit, I'm glad he wants to be a father to her. She deserves that."

"She is my daughter." I tried to control my rage. "I'm the only father she wants and the only one she needs. I don't give a damn if he's the president, she is still my kid, Sands."

"Well where the hell were you when she needed you last night, daddy dearest?"

"I don't have time to do this with you Cassandra." I gritted my teeth.

"Look, all I want you to do is talk to her." She quickly pulled herself together and lowered her voice. "She listens to you Eddie. God only knows why."

She had reverted to being nice again, at least as nice as she knew how to be with me. She hated the thought of having to ask me for anything at all, so I knew things had to be difficult to make her do something she despised.

"Will you please talk to her, Gitz?"

"Sure Sands, whatever," I finally caved in. "Can you bring her by my place later?"

"Actually I was hoping you could come by the house this evening." She bit down on her lip.

"You mean with you and Robert?" I raised an eyebrow.

"I just think that if she sees how comfortable you are with Robert and me, she'll get used to the idea." She fidgeted again.

I stared back at her. "Who said I was comfortable with it?"

"Eddie, please!!"

"All right, I'll be there."

***

I found Lou three floors above in District Attorney Nelson Peters' office. Nelson resembled his father in a lot of ways. He had the same pocked face and greasy hair. He had an average build, and that pretty much summed up his personality as well, just average. Nelson had devoted the better part of his life to becoming a stalwart pillar of the community. He made the ideal public servant. All the while trying to lay to rest the fact that his father, my old partner, was a bad cop. Yet another sour taste of yesterday.

"Ah, Mr. Gideon, so nice of you to drop by," Nelson grinned. "Saves me the trouble of having you brought in to answer questions."

"Nice to see you too, Nelson. I've got a few questions of my own. Unfortunately, most of them are for Lou." I admired the cut of his suit. "City must be paying you good."

"I'm grateful for the things my position affords me. I'm glad you have a sense of humor, Eddie. For a man in your position, it's a good thing to have." He bounced his cool stare back and forth between Lou and me. "Now officially, I can't promise you anything of course, but if you cooperate, there may be some room for leniency. That is, if you've come to make a statement."

"You really think you've got me?" I smiled.

"Oh, I know I've got you this time, Gideon." He pointed at me. "It's just a matter of putting all the pieces together, lining up all the shit we've got on you and burying you in it. You won't slip through this time. You murdered Carole Spenser and I know you did it."

"All this attention is starting to make me feel all warm inside," I picked up a pen from his desk. "You seem to have taken a personal interest in this case, Nelson. I wonder what the press will say when the story hits the streets. Ought to be pretty interesting considering our past history, don't you think?"

That stupid smile crept across his face again. "Like I said, no cons, no tricks, and no word to the press until we're ready to hang you out to dry. Rest assured I'll be there every step of the way. But if you're wondering whether or not I'm stupid enough to get into the spotlight with you to help you gain some kind of sympathy, I've got a surprise for you."

The look in Lou's eyes told me even he wasn't sure what the hell Nelson was talking about. Confident little bastard, you had to give him that. So what did he have up his sleeve that had him in such a self-assured state?

"Becky, please send J.T. in here?" He spat into his intercom.

"Right away, sir," a voice replied.

Lou stared at him. "Who the hell is J.T.?"

Nelson's attention focused on the sound at the door. You could feel the absolute glee in his voice as he threw out his invitation to join us in his office. My heart jumped in my throat as a woman entered Nelson's office then shut the door behind her. I watched her legs as she glided across the room to Nelson's side, the look on her face, innocent and unassuming. The name escaped me, but the face I knew.

Nelson grinned. "Gentlemen, allow me to introduce to you the woman who'll be handling this case, the new A.D.A., Jordan Taylor McCrae."

NINE

L ou nervously crossed in front of me to shake Jordan's hand. Her eyes scanned back and forth from Lou to Nelson before they rested on me again. Nelson sat back at his desk, fondling a paperweight, looking quite pleased with himself. Son-of-a-bitch. I wondered if he had sent her to Deacon's the night I ran into her. Did he know we knew each other? Was that why he was so smug?

"Mr. Gideon is our prime suspect in the Carole Spenser case," he smiled at her.

Jordan looked a bit puzzled for some reason, as though all of this came as something of a surprise to her.

"Mr. Gideon?" she stammered. She didn't let on we had met before.

"Counselor." I held my hand out to shake hers. "Should I have my attorney here?"

"I wasn't under the impression that this was a formal inquiry." She gripped my hand briefly, glaring over my shoulder at Nelson. "If you're uncomfortable about this meeting, perhaps we should wait for your attorney, just to make sure we're all up front here."

"Mr. Gideon was just here to speak with the Lieutenant." Nelson jumped in quickly. "I thought it would help things along for everyone involved to meet."

Jordan didn't seem to be buying into Nelson's answer. But I wasn't about to let my guard down with Jordan just yet. I sensed some tension between her and Nelson, but whether they had staged it for my benefit or just didn't like one another, I'd have to tackle that later.

"Well, as the good District Attorney said, we all had to meet sometime, just so we know who all the players are." I turned to Nelson again. "Although I have to admit, now that I know who I'm up against, I'll definitely have to take this matter more seriously."

"As well you should," Nelson nodded.

"I'm glad Ms. McCrae will be keeping things on the up and up, knowing how we both feel about honesty and respect. I'm glad she's in charge." I headed for the door. "You know where to find me Nelson, and if not, I'm sure the new A.D.A. can cover for you."

I kept a smile on my face all the way to the elevator. Lou caught up with me there and we rode down together. I started to wonder if the D.A. really had something to tie me to Carole's murder. Maybe they'd found the murder weapon. Even though I'd taken care not to show it, the sight of Jordan coming into Nelson's office shook me some. I felt like the kid in school everyone whispered about. You knew people were talking about you, but you couldn't hear what they said. Stuff like that made me nervous and when I get nervous, I exit.

"What the hell was that honesty and respect crap about?" Lou glared at me. "Why are you trying to push that kid's button?"

"Because he's trying to push mine," I snapped back. "He's a smartass, anyway, why should I give a damn about him?"

"Because that smart ass is the D.A., and no matter how much of a prick he is, he can still make your life hell."

"Does he have anything on me?" I asked.

"Nelson blows more smoke than a fan in a forest fire. He's got what we've got, which don't amount to shit right now. That's why you're not sitting in a cell and that's why the press hasn't gotten wind of this yet. But I gotta tell you Gitz, he's putting the pressure on us to nail you to this."

"What else is new?" I checked my jaw again to see if there was any swelling.

"Damn." I winced in pain.

"What the hell happened to you?"

"I ran into Derek Simmons' fist." My whole face hurt.

"You two had a fight?" His eyes lit up. "Where?"

"His office. I found out he and Carole used to work together at Prentiss Securities and he knew who I was and that I was seeing Carole."

"How'd that happen?"

I glared at him now. "You tell me, Lou."

He shook his head. "Uh-uh, no way anybody at the crime scene told him who you are. He left not long after you did. Maybe Carole told him."

"I'm still wondering about that myself." I watched Lou reach into his coat pocket and grab a pack of cigarettes. "Thought you gave those things up?"

Lou gave me a cold look as he flipped one in his mouth and searched for a light. His fingers fumbled with his lighter which I finally took and lit for him.

"Thanks." He took a deep puff on his cigarette and then exhaled slowly. "I don't like the way this whole thing is panning out, Gitz. You've got a long list of enemies who'd love to frame you for murder."

"That tends to happen when you're a cop who puts honesty and the law above department loyalty."

"Right, but most of them aren't cold-blooded murderers. So who do you think hated Carole Spenser enough to want her dead?" He took another long pull and exhaled a plume of smoke.

"My first guess would be Derek Simmons, but I'm not ready to commit to that yet until I've got some proof."

"There isn't anything you haven't told me about is there, Gitz?" He puffed again.

"What makes you say that?"

"Just checking to see if there's anything you might want to tell me before this thing goes too far." He reached the stub filter now. "Look, you've come out pretty straight considering all the screw-ups you've made. I just don't want to see you throw away what little you got left, y'know?"

"You gonna run out and buy me card, Lou?" I smiled.

"I'm gonna kick you in the teeth if you don't stop being such a smart-ass!" He stuck his finger in my face. "Don't make me come down on you. I want to know where you are at all times for the next 24 hours."

"Well, I'm on my way home to get some things together and then I'm heading over to the house for dinner," I said.

That made him stop for a moment.

"You mean you and Sands?" The cigarette fell out of his mouth and onto the floor. I stomped it out before anyone could notice. "What's going on with that?"

"Nothing, we just need to talk, that's all."

He grinned. "Well talking is good. Nice to see you kids working things out. You gotta learn to put the past behind you."

"Don't grow hair on me, Lou." I ushered him toward the exit. "It's just dinner, and no there's not a snowball's chance in hell we're getting back together."

"You're a real screw-up for letting her go, y'know."

"And you're a real jackass for reminding me," I said.

TEN

I made sure Lou was well out of sight before I went back into the building. I didn't want him with me when I went down to see Skip. He had an attitude about the man. The nausea had subsided but my head pain was coming in waves now. The frigid corridors in the courthouse basement chilled my exposed flesh, the temperature just slightly above forty degrees. It reminded me of my Aunt Ida's basement, cold, dank, and full of tiny crawly things that defied description and unsettled the stomach. Hard to tell if my goosebumps were from the temperature or the creepy environment.

The peeling paint and inadequate lighting made for an eerie effect. Visions of old horror movies with unsuspecting young coeds about to meet an excruciating end crept into my mind. An astringent smell filled the air. A mixture of pine cleaner and bleach that made your eyes water if you stood in one place for too long. I rounded the corner to another hallway, refreshingly better ventilated than the first. The air felt even cooler but the bleach smell had faded.

As I entered the Medical Examiner's office, I encountered two women. One sat at a desk while the other hovered just above her, pointing down at a magazine. They both had jet black hair, straight and shiny. The woman standing wore her hair shorter, in a marquis cut, while the other wore hers long, like something I'd seen in some vampire movie. Neither woman seemed to notice me as I entered. Something held their attention as they ogled the page in front of them.

"Excuse me." I tried to appear polite. "I'm looking for Skip."

The one sitting looked up at me. Her eyes widened suddenly as though I'd surprised her. She was pale, skin almost bone white, with dark eye makeup. Her was face round and came to a point at her chin. I guessed her to be in her twenties and certainly sure of herself from the look in her eyes.

"What's your name?"

"Tell him Gitz is here." I shook off the look she gave me.

The woman standing behind her looked me over; the way you'd look at a steak in the supermarket. Like her friend, she was pale and thin. She wore a T-shirt that was painfully stretched against her bosom. She threw her head back, giving me the once over in detail. Her tongue slid between her lips and rested in the corner of her mouth as she brought her forefinger against her nose. I wasn't sure whether I liked being ogled the way they did it.

"Something not to your liking?" I stared back.

"What's not to like?" Her eyes seemed focused on something other than mine. "What's your name again?"

"Eddie Gideon. Where's Skip?" My patience had grown thin.

"I thought you said your name was Gitz?" The seated one smiled.

"My friends call me Gitz," I returned.

The standing one approached me. "I like that name Gitz, it kind of suits you. This is Liza and my name is Vicki." She reached down and took my hand, her fingers making tiny circles on my skin. "You've got soft hands for a man, you party?"

I knew she wasn't speaking of the kind of party I generally attended. She stroked my hand with a long, pointed fingernail, sending shivers up my arm. I took a moment to respond to her question. Her dark eyes seemed to suck me in by the throat. Not that I didn't appreciate the gesture, but the morgue was the last place I'd ever want to have a sexual experience. God, why did I attract these strange women to me?

Just then, Skip appeared from a room behind them. He still had earbuds in his ears. His eyes widened as he noticed me.

"Gitz, what brings you to hell?" He smiled, exposing those long white teeth.

"We need to talk." I sighed. "You got a few minutes?"

"I take it you met my assistants?" Skip threw a glance over to Liza and Vicki.

"We just met," I nodded.

"If it's okay with you Skip, Liza and I are going to take a break." Vicki offered in her most professional tone. "Anything you need while we're out?"

"Just coffee for now, Vicki. I got a feeling I'll be up all night again." Skip handed her a five-dollar bill.

Liza slid from behind her desk and smiled as she moved past me. Vicki on the other hand, made it a point to get as close to me as possible as she passed by. "I really enjoyed meeting you, Gitz." She accentuated my name.

"Uh, likewise," I shuddered.

I found myself staring at them as they left the room, wondering what devious little diversions she might have had planned for me if given the opportunity. Behind me I could hear Skip chuckling to himself with immense pleasure. I suddenly got the feeling that I had been set-up by the little rat bastard.

"What's so damn funny?"

"God, I hope you aren't planning on trying to date Vicki."

"Not that I was, but what makes you ask?" I turned to face him.

"Well, she's not your type of woman," he laughed, removing his ear-buds.

"Oh really? Please enlighten me. What's my type of woman?"

"Oh... you know. Straight. Cis. Goes out in the daylight. Doesn't leave bite marks—except for the alimony."

"Sounds like you know me well," I scoffed. "God, you make me sound so conventional and...old."

"Well, you're sounding more and more like Lieutenant Lard Ass every day. Where is the jolly mean cop anyway?" He reached into his lab coat pocket and pulled out a square case.

"Where he should be, which is not here." I sighed. "I need a favor from you."

"Name it." He put his earbuds in the case, dropped it in his pocket, and pulled out a stick of gum. I waited as he unwrapped it and popped it in his mouth.

"I want to see Carole Spenser's body."

He stopped, mid-chew. "You want to see the body? Gitz, you can't be serious."

"I need to see the body, Skip. Don't ask why."

He began chewing his gum again. "I dunno, Gitz. I mean, normally there wouldn't be a problem but..."

"But what? Did you lose the body or something?" I threw his own humor back at him. Skip looked anything but jovial now.

"Look, there's no easy way to say this, Eddie. We've already done an autopsy on the body. I just finished an hour ago. She's not so good to look at right now, okay?" Skip stumbled about for a proper explanation.

I hadn't thought about the autopsy or that it might've already been completed. The thought of him cutting into her body jolted me a bit. Though I'd never viewed one up close and personal, I knew from the way his eyebrows drew together Skip worried about how I might react to the sight of her mutilated body.

"What if I just looked at her face?"

"Gitz, I'm trying to do you a favor for real here." Skip seemed determined now. "You don't want to go down there."

"I've got to see her one more time, Skip." I almost begged him. "Just let me look at her one more time. I need that right now."

He stood face to face with me. "You don't have to be a genius to know that going down there and seeing her lying cold on that table is gonna seriously mess with your mind. Do you need that?" he asked.

"Someone else decided for me when they killed her." I leaned against the desk. "Somebody walked in and killed her with me lying next to her. My mind has already been messed with. Right now I'm trying to get my soul back."

"You really cared for her, huh?" His eyes widened.

I didn't know if I could answer his question. Admitting to Skip that I loved her now would only make her death that much harder to deal with. My concentration felt weak enough without the burden of a total emotional upheaval. I had to stay focused on what I had to do.

"No matter how things turn out, a part of me will always feel responsible for what happened. I don't know if this will help me, but it's something I have to do. Yeah, I had feelings for her." I confessed.

Skip didn't say a word as he turned to guide me down another dim hallway. His slow and deliberate steps made me wonder if he hoped I'd suddenly change my mind and ask him more about Liza and Vicki. But my mind had gone elsewhere, tunneling through what I remembered of the last time I saw Carole alive, trying to sift through all the passion and discover reason where none existed.

We paused in front of two huge metal doors. He looked me in the eye, then swiped his badge to open the doors. We entered a room with two huge sinks on either side of another door which was sealed at the bottom by black rubber tubing. Warnings to scrub immediately after exiting the storage area covered the walls, reducing the risk of any dormant infections that might escape.

Skip went to my right, reached in a drawer, and pulled out a pair of surgical masks, eyewear, and a gown for me to wear. He still hadn't said a word as he helped me get into the protective wear. He tied it in three places along my spine, then handed me gloves and shoe covers. He snapped on his own gloves and shoe covers.

"Is all this really necessary?" I asked.

"Even though you're wearing gloves, you must keep your hands away from the table at all times. I don't want you picking up anything." His clinical, stern answer reminded me of the school nurse in junior high. He paused in front of the last door and turned to me again, his protective eyewear riding his forehead and the surgical mask below his chin.

"Gitz, are you sure?"

I'd seen my share of corpses in the line of duty, but he was right, this was different. All of a sudden my hands grew cold and trembled, but I nodded for him to continue.

"Let's go." Skip sighed, then pulled his eyewear over his eyes and brought the mask up over his mouth.

A rush of cool air surrounded us as Skip pushed through the door and ushered me inside. Long humming florescent bulbs doused us with harsh, bright light. Stainless steel with three tiers of matching doors measuring three feet-by-four covered the wall to our right. A table stood in the center of the room. Behind it I saw a desk with a lamp and a half-eaten sandwich. God, how could anyone eat in here?

The same astringent smell I met in the corridor engulfed the room, some kind of special cleaning solution. At the far end of the table, sat a small desk with a computer, a tablet, and a couple of cameras. Along the opposite wall, there were a number of machines, instruments, and tools. I shuddered to guess what they might be used for.

Skip walked alongside the stainless-steel wall, running his hand against each of the doors he passed. Every now and then he'd glance over his shoulder to make sure I hadn't ducked out on him. He went over to the desk and picked up the tablet. He tapped it a couple of times, then slowly scrolled the digital report, studying it and me with a peculiar intensity. He hiked himself up on the desk and let out an annoying sigh. What the hell was he up to?

"How much did you know about this woman, Gitz?" He kept his eyes focused on the screen.

"How do you mean?"

"What did you know about her past?"

"Are you trying to tell me she had some sexually transmitted disease?" I frowned. "I did use condoms."

Skip actually laughed, but obviously my answer didn't match his thoughts. He threw the tablet down on the desk and moved in front of one of the stainless-steel doors. He paused and lowered his head briefly, as though offering up a prayer. Skip praying in any sense, didn't fit what I knew of him. But then, we never discussed his religious beliefs.

"Here we go," he murmured.

With a jerk he pulled open the door which slid out effortlessly between the two of us.

Skip guided the door with his hand until he had completely opened the case, revealing a body covered by a sheet. The muscles in his neck strained as he laid his hand upon the sheet. I suddenly found myself unable to stand still. Skip gave me a clinical stare. I crossed my arms in front of me and nodded for him to continue.

Skip pulled back the sheet from her head to her collarbone. I gripped the edge of the metal as a familiar surge of nausea returned.

His voice was slightly muffled by the mask as he began giving me the facts from the autopsy report. "Subject is a Black female, dark hair, green eyes, approximately 32 years of age. Subject died as a result of a bullet entering the left breast, severing the thoracic aorta, and causing massive internal bleeding. The angle of the wound suggests the bullet entered the body upward at a 45-degree angle and lodged against the spinal column." His tone sounded artificial, clinical.

It didn't look like Carole at all. Her soft features had become lifeless and pale, her lips deep purple-grey and stiff as twigs in autumn. Why did it suddenly seem like a lifetime ago I had held this woman in my arms when time had only passed in the space of days? This corpse had once been a beautiful vibrant woman, but it wasn't the Carole I knew. I felt my heart beating in my throat as I stared down at her motionless face and ragged hair with dried blood in it.

"There is some soft tissue damage in the area of the neck and two cervical vertebrae fractures, suggesting that the body was struck by a forceful blow."

It took every ounce of strength within me to keep from touching her. I wanted to run my fingers against the dark line that cut its way around her neck, the result of where it had been broken according to Skip's findings. My hands trembled at the edge of the metal slab. I could no longer fight off the tears. I turned away quickly before Skip could notice, but then maybe it didn't really matter what he saw. Doing what he did, he'd no doubt seen worse. It tore me apart inside to see her this way, to think I could have done something to prevent this.

"The autopsy also revealed that the deceased had recently used a large quantity of amphetamines and cocaine." Skip reported. "Further analysis showed that the deceased used these drugs on a regular basis."

"Wait a minute. You're saying Carole used drugs?" I stammered, turning to face him.

"I'm not saying anything." He pulled the sheet back over her face. "Her blood tests came back screaming of it. She was so lit up I could've started a fire with what she was on. I'm not even gonna tell you some of the places she used to shoot up."

I shook my head defiantly. "No way, Skip. You must have screwed up somewhere. Carole never took as much as an aspirin in front of me. How could she have been using?"

"In front of you? Look, just because she was on drugs, doesn't mean she was a slouch about it." He threw his arms out to his sides. "People in corporate positions snort and pop pills all the time to stay on top of their game. These days it's more the rule than the exception. You can find more drugs in the workplace than you can on the street."

"Skip, I spent more than a few nights with this woman. We'd been dating for months." I shook my head. "If she'd been on something, I'd have known."

"Did you follow her into the toilet every time she excused herself?" he inquired. "Did you help her park the car every time or see her to her office every morning? Look, all I'm saying is that it only takes a minute to get high. You could turn your head and she'd pop a pill before you'd know what was on the menu. Hell, I know poppers so good, they'll snort in front of a cop just for kicks."

I found this all a little hard to swallow. Had Carole really hidden a substance abuse problem from me? I'd never seen her with so much as a prescribed bottle of pills, let alone any narcotics. But I hadn't been with Carole every single moment of the day, and the fact that in all the times we had seen one another, that I'd never been to her apartment until that night bothered me more. What did I really know about this woman? Was I so swept up in the heat of romance that I didn't see what was going on around me? God, could I be that blind? Maybe Skip was right that she needed just a quick moment to get her fix.

I shook my head. "None of this makes any sense."

"Don't beat yourself up over it, Gitz. Like I said, she was really good at it," Skip began slowly returning the body to its cell. "If it's any consolation, she was probably doing the drugs to deal with all the pain from the cancer."

"What cancer?"

Skip's eyes slowly swelled like dough rising in the oven. His lips trembled and faltered as though his motor skills had suddenly taken a holiday. He turned away for a second, putting his face and thoughts in order. "I'm sorry Gitz, I thought you knew about it. It appears to have started in her breast, but then it spread."

I stared down at the sheet. "How long?" I whispered.

Skip drew a deep breath. "I can't say, but from the way it had spread, I don't think she'd have lasted very long."

Skip allowed me to draw the sheet from Carole's face once more. Even with her lying there, I could almost hear her ask me why I had let this happen to her. I could almost feel her leaning against me, wondering what I was going to do about it. Instinctively, I raised my hand to stroke her cheek, but Skip stopped me, shaking his head slowly. A chill went through me like nothing I'd ever known before. Carole was dead. I just wanted to put my hand against her face one last time and embrace the unbearable pain as it sucked the life from my soul. I wanted to remember this moment and be able to extract it from my memory when I stood face to face with Carole's killer. I wanted to share it with him when I brought him to his knees.

ELEVEN

I drove around the block twice before I finally turned into my former driveway. I didn't know why, maybe to see if Cassandra had invited some of her nosy friends over so they could all take a few potshots at me for old times' sake, especially Anna Katz. Anna lived across the street from us on Winchester. Her dark wood shingled house stuck out like a sore thumb on our street and looked like a rotten apple somebody left on the grocery shelf too long.

She was tending her yard when I drove up, eyeing me inquisitively as she watered her flowers. Everyone believed Anna to be in her forties, though she told the whole neighborhood she was thirty-two. A whiny bore, she stood approximately five-foot-nine without the benefit of heels. She tanned often, too often, which would explain her constantly peeling skin. Anna knew more about everyone's business than most people knew about themselves. She had a nasty habit of always dropping by with some grave news that could affect the community. Her grandiose excuse to gossip with a vengeance. How I've wished at times that she were a man, and even then, I wondered would anyone care too much about me punching her out.

I stood in the drive for a moment admiring the house Cassandra and I built, a modest two-story with a cobblestone face and spacious front yard. We planted an apple tree in the yard the week Stephie was born and I was still waiting for a decent couple of bites. Geraniums lined the walk to the door. On the mailbox, perched just to the right of the door, Cassandra had scribbled in "MS." in front of our name.

Cassandra's famous wall of flowers obstructed the view of the family room. Large hanging plants and vines crawled against long thin wood slabs hiding the antique breakfront that sat near the window. I peeked through the door glass to see what she had moved out or around in the last few years. At least she kept the dog, Mooch. It felt funny ringing the doorbell to the house I still made payments on. I stuck my hands in my pockets and listened to the shuffle of feet against linoleum. I hoped dearly Robert wouldn't be the one answering the door, welcoming me to their home.

"Dad!" Stephie's eyes lit up my heart.

I barely caught her as she leaped into my arms.

"It's so good to see you!" She threw her arms around as much of me as she could before bringing them to rest around my neck.

I missed those hazel brown eyes and her giddiness. Stephie was fast growing into a woman. Twelve years old with the grace of a gymnast and the moxie not to take any crap from anyone. She had come up a few inches since I saw her last. She reached about five-foot-six now and she'd let her hair go long and billowy. She looked increasingly like her mother.

"How's my baby girl?" I tried not to let my emotions get the best of me. "You staying out of trouble?"

She gave me a discerning look, her eyebrows drawn together on her face as though I should have known better than to ask. Then she hugged me again and pulled me into the house. The smell of mint in the foyer almost burned the eyes. Cassandra had a thing for every room having its own scent, ambience she called it. Bullshit, I thought.

"I was worried when you didn't show up last night. I figured you must have been working on a case or something. Mom says she saw you down at the courthouse today, are you in some kind of trouble?" Stephie's eyes asked me to reassure her.

I squinted and tried to return the look she had given me. She giggled and suddenly we stood there trying to tickle one another. She finally surrendered as I caved in on her and left her screaming on the floor.

"What the hell is going on?" Cassandra barked from upstairs.

"Nothing!" Stephie yelled back between guffaws.

"Well you better keep it down, young lady!" Cassandra called back.

"Yeah, just like Roberto keeps you down." Stephie snickered.

"What was that?"

"Nothing!" she hollered.

I tried to smother a smile. "That wasn't very nice."

"His parents weren't very nice for naming him Robert Ernest Macy. What a geek." She made a beeline for the living room with me in tow. Stephie liked to dish the dirt on old Robert. "So how come you're coming over for dinner? Mom on your case again?"

"Can't I just drop by to see you on a whim?"

"Dad, get real. You don't grow up in a cop's house, hang out with cops' kids and not have it rub off on you."

"You're a real piece of work, kiddo," I laughed.

"Smart ass, problem child, disturbed youth. God, you old people live by these labels don't you?" She had become a little too good at this.

"You're gettin' a mouth on you, too. I don't know which is worse, arguing with you or your mother."

"Like, me, I'm sure." She pouted in an irritating valley girl tone. "What's going on, Dad?"

"Okay." I sighed. "First, I came to apologize for last night. I got caught up in something I couldn't get out of. And I promise I'll make it up to you."

"It's okay, really. What else?"

"What's going on with you and Robert?" I inquired.

Her eyes suddenly narrowed and she glared back out into the foyer again. "She told you didn't she? What a witch!"

"Hey!" I leaned in close. "You don't have to like her boyfriend. But she's still your mother Stephie, she deserves your respect."

"Do you know they're planning to get married?" she whined. "He's such a total jerk. All he could talk about all day was how we were going to be such a happy family and about the people he knew at my school and how he could help me out."

"But you realize he and your mother are going to be married and that means he'll be living here with you." I couldn't believe I was actually defending this worm. "You'll only be hurting your mom if you don't at least try to get along."

"To hell with him and her," she hissed.

"Hey, I'm not kidding about respecting your mom, Stephie. And I never gave you permission to use that kind of language with me either, so cool it." I could hear myself sounding like a parent.

"Sorry, Dad," she said just above a whisper. Then she gave me the sad-eyed look. "I just don't like it when they talk about you, saying you don't want to spend time with me. I know it's hard for you to be with me more 'cause you and mom fight a lot, and I know what they said about you isn't true, but it hurts. I don't like anybody messing with my Dad."

Stephie did her best to catch her tears before they ran down her face. She turned and tried to compose herself, wanting so desperately to be tough for me. I sat there silently for a moment, hoping she wouldn't turn around and see me crying either. For all of thirty seconds I cried a little, about me, about Stephie, at last for Carole. I couldn't help but think of all the times I told her about Stephie and how I wanted her to meet my little girl someday. Stephie made me realize just how much I would miss her. She also made me realize what my indiscretion had cost me, my home, and my family. Why didn't I think of these times when I wasn't being a faithful husband? Hindsight could really be a bitch when you're staring into the eyes of a twelve-year-old wonder who loves you no matter what you've done.

I pulled her into my arms. "Stephanie Nicole, I love you more than anything in the world."

"More than the Browns?"

"More than a trip to the Super Bowl," I laughed. "And I will always be your father. Don't ever doubt that I wouldn't do anything in the world for you. I'll tell you something, no matter what happens between your mom and me, I'm always there for you, always loving you even when I'm not around."

"Even if I want you to take me to a heavy metal concert?"

"So long as the guys don't wear lipstick," I teased.

"All right, I'll try and be nice to Roberto," she agreed.

"Well that's good news," Cassandra came into the living room and studied us both carefully. She wore a green and red sequined evening dress and high heels. Who the hell did she expect for dinner anyway? "Stephie, shouldn't you be getting changed for dinner?"

"Go ahead Stephie, I want to talk to your mom anyway," I said before they could get into it.

Stephie gave me a peck, running past Cassandra without a word.

"What's on your mind, Sands?"

"Everything go okay with you and Stephie?" she asked.

"Yes I talked to her like you asked, not that I needed to, but she's trying to adjust. I just hope that you and Robert will remember that," I said sternly.

She smiled. "Well, I suppose I should thank you, Eddie."

I could feel myself start to boil over.

"You don't owe me anything Sands, in fact, I wouldn't bother setting a place for me at your dinner table either. God, what the hell were you thinking?" I couldn't keep the anger out of my voice.

"What are you talking about?"

"Stephie told me about how you and Robert have been telling her that I don't want to spend time with her. Is it true, are you really that cruel? Or did you think she'd just believe whatever the two of you conjured up without question?" I shouted.

"And when was the last time you were there when she needed a father, Eddie? How many times in the last month have you come by without me calling you? At least Robert tries, at least he's willing to be the kind of father our daughter needs!"

"How the hell would you know what kind of father she needs, Cassandra? Who died and made you God?"

Tears welled in her eyes. "You did. The day you walked out that door you left me to be mother and father to our child. How dare you condemn me for trying to give us both a better life? Robert may not meet your expectations of what Stephie needs in a father, but at least he wants us, at least he wants me."

I could feel my heart pounding as the tears rolled down Cassandra's face. After all this time, we were still fighting the same battle, a useless struggle over who loved who more, and who didn't. I hadn't come here to mess with her life. I'd done a superb job of that already. But she knew how much I loved Stephie and she had no right to do what she did.

"Let me make this as clear as I can for you Sands, nobody is going to replace me as Stephie's father, not now, not ever." I shook my finger in her face.

The knock at the door cut our argument short. I decided to answer the door on my own. Robert looked a bit surprised to see me standing there and not quite sure what to make of it. And that felt good.

"Uh, Eddie." He cleared his throat. "Nice to see you again."

He held out his hand to me.

Robert was tall and pale, in his early forties and wore a well-kept beard that he couldn't help playing with when he was nervous. Robert consoled his way into Cassandra's broken heart like the usual garden variety snake, which meant of course he had no backbone.

"So, Sandra tells me you'll be joining us for dinner."

"Unfortunately, I can't stay." I knew he'd be relieved to hear that.

"What about Stephie?" Cassandra had pulled herself together.

"Since you seem to like telling her about me, you can tell her that I'm sorry I had to leave, but I'll drop by again in a couple of days to see how she's doing." I leered.

"Just make sure you call first." She faked a smile.

"By the way Robert, I understand congratulations are in order." I took his hand and squeezed it firmly. "I know the two of you will be happy together."

"Gee Eddie, thanks. I really appreciate it," he smiled.

"And one more thing," I could hear his labored breathing as I stepped closer to his ear. "If I hear that you bad mouthed me in front of my daughter again, I'll do things to your face your insurance doesn't cover, okay?" I patted him a little too hard on the shoulder. "Well, goodnight all."

I didn't know if Cassandra heard what I'd said to Robert and I really didn't care. I just hoped he didn't think I was crawling back to her. That would really be a crime. But as much as I would have loved to give them both a piece of my mind, I knew things with Cassandra would get ugly again and I couldn't do that to my kid. And there was another problem, I couldn't forget about Carole and the fact that her death had left me as the prime suspect.

I looked up at the house again and caught sight of Stephie, standing in the window. She nodded to me, letting me know she understood, just the way she always had. I felt sorry for all the trouble my split with Cassandra caused them both. Being a bi-racial child was hard enough, the divorce didn't make things any easier for her. But like she said, you can't grow up being a cop's kid without it rubbing off on you a little. Stephie would be fine, of that much I was certain. I waved and blew her a kiss as I turned away.

I sat in my car, staring at the shoebox of letters I took from Carole's apartment. I wasn't sure why I'd taken them or why I felt the need to carry them around for that matter. Officially they were still considered evidence and should have been handed over to the police. But then, breaking rules and giving policy and procedure the finger could be a good thing every now and then. God, I was beginning to remind myself of Skip.

As I pulled out of the driveway, I noticed a light come on in the house across the street and saw Anna Katz peeking out of one corner of her curtains. Being a kind courteous neighbor, I couldn't think of leaving without acknowledging her. So I gave her the finger.

TWELVE

By the time I got back to my place it was well after eight and I felt hungry enough to have eaten my mail. I sifted through the day's deposit of bills as I checked voicemail. There were three messages, two from Lou, warning me to steer clear of Derek Simmons, who claimed I had harassed him. The third was Nicole from Dr. Kamen's office asking me to give them a call as soon as possible.

I called down and asked John to put something on a plate for me and have one of the girls bring it up. Tempting as the crowd downstairs sounded, I knew better than to end the day without jotting down some notes. I searched my phone and discovered that the address I found with Cappie's name on it was for a place called Sommerville Retirement Community. And of all the things on my list, telling Cappie about Carole seemed to have an urgency of its own.

In the bottom of one of my file cabinets I kept a stack of maps for every state east of the Mississippi. These things came in handy when you're fumbling around on some dark road in the middle of the sticks, out of range of any cell towers. I'd only been to Illinois once, so the map still looked fairly new, which meant I hadn't scribbled all over the damn thing.

I traced the directions from my phone onto the paper map and I booked a cab, a flight, and a rental car for early the next morning. My Camaro would sit in its usual parking spot at home, and if I timed everything right, nobody would know that I had left town.

"Knock, knock. Is it alright to come in?" Rita didn't bother to wait for an answer. She wore a red and white polka dot dress with a matching scarf in her hair. The blush on her cheeks didn't quite match her ensemble, but Rita preferred off the wall as standard decor.

"John sent up the chicken and red beans." She ushered the warm plate to my desk. "Personally, I would have brought you the vegetarian plate, better for you anyway."

"Thanks Rita, I'll get to it in a minute." I was distracted with tomorrow's plans. Where did I put that travel bag?

"Things going okay with you, Gitz?" She seemed to be fishing for something. "I've been getting these bad vibes all day."

"Bad vibes?" I smiled at her precociously. "You mean you weren't eavesdropping on me and John the other day?"

Rita hated it when I saw through her veil of mysticism. It forced her to deal with me on my level, talk and act like the rest of us. Something she seldom did.

"Look Eddie, I like you—as a friend I mean," she quickly corrected. "It doesn't take a psychic to see your girlfriend's death is really doing a number on you. The other night you were moody as shit and you didn't even say a word to half the staff. It's not like you, Gitz. I just want to help if I can."

"Look, I'm sorry if I came off rough the other night. I haven't been feeling myself lately."

"Is it true they think you killed her?"

I nodded and looked over the food on my desk.

"How could someone do something like that while you slept?"

"Same question I been asking myself for the last couple of days, Rita. How could I let it happen?" I hadn't been comfortable talking about this with John but talking about Carole with Rita came easy. "How could I let her get killed?"

"Eddie, I didn't mean to insinuate that you—"

"—I know, I know." I turned away from her now. "And you're right. This whole mess has really done a number on me. The worse part of it is I'm not sure what happened that night."

"Is there anything I can do?" she offered weakly.

"Tell me what happened that night, tell me who killed Carole." I whispered.

"Eddie, I'm sorry." Her voice cracked with genuine sadness.

I walked over to Rita and gave her a big hug. She meant well, but Rita was extremely emotional and if I didn't end this now she'd start crying and never leave. It took some doing but I managed to convince her I would be fine.

***

I told John where I'd be and he promised to cover in case anyone started asking for me. The cab was late so I arrived at the airport just after five-thirty a.m. with thirty minutes to spare before my flight boarded. It took ten minutes at the check-in kiosk, eleven minutes through security, and another six to get to the gate. In the three minutes I had left, a funny thought crossed my mind. It struck me that during my time on the force, I'd never done a Death Notification. I'd been on a few where another officer had to tell some poor guy's family that he'd died, but I never actually had to say the words myself, look them in the eye as they crumbled into shrieking sobs. No amount of kindness in your voice could prepare them for that kind of shock.

Surprisingly enough, Sommerville, which was actually the name of a town, wasn't the rural backwash I thought it might turn out to be. Most places I've been to that end in "Ville" are usually communities where the people are trying to get back to a simpler time. They always reminded me of those B movies where the stranger stops in for a drink and gets caught up in the town's problems.

The town was only ninety minutes' drive from the airport and the fresh air helped clear my thoughts a bit. My paper map came in handy when cell service grew spotty. When I booked it, I made a point of making sure my rental car had a CD player. I packed a few discs fearing what I might find on the satellite radio. Skip had put together a little collection of stuff to wean me on in the progressive vein. Most of the bizarre stuff I just zoomed past, except for one remake of "White Rabbit" which I played several times over and over again. The one song I found most intriguing was by a group called Concrete Blonde; odd since the lead singer, from Skip's report, had coal black hair. It was a song called "Caroline."

I pulled into the first eatery along the road leading into town, one of those family-owned burger shops that had likely been around since they founded the town. The building had an odd shape, sloped and receding into the ground the closer you came to the back of it. I almost expected a couple of gnomes to stroll out with aprons on. A jolly woman with deep-set dimples welcomed me to Mackie's and took my take-out order.

She whipped the ticket around to a freckled faced kid working his ass off over a hot grill. It was close to 85 degrees outside, so it had to be nearly

100 in the kitchen. Bernice, my new-found friend at the counter gave me some quickie back road directions to the retirement community and ten minutes later I left with my food. I dropped a five for a tip and bought the kid behind the grill a soda. Not even a kid should have to work that hard.

Two miles and a dozen fries later, I careened onto a cobblestone drive and paused before a gate where an unpleasant looking guard waved me in his general direction. I could hear his heavy breathing as he lifted himself from a wavering stool and made his way to me. Unlike Bernice at the burger place, this man didn't carry his weight well. His cheeks looked like large dollops of sagging dough, pink and burned by the sun. His stomach rolled over his belt so deeply that it took him two or three heaves just to get his pants up where he could walk comfortably.

"Can I help you, mister?" He panted between breaths.

"I'm here to visit someone, a Charles Coleman." I offered him my credentials. "I'm a private investigator. I have to see him about his grand-daughter."

He gave me a smarmy look before he handed me back my ID and then with a wave, he instructed me to follow the drive to the administration building and they would tell me where I could find Cappie. I sighed in relief, glad to be down wind of the smell of his armpits. In the back of my mind I wondered if he slid down to Mackie's to munch a few before going home to dinner. For Bernice's sake I prayed she didn't see this guy often.

I didn't know who owned this retirement community, but it looked so nice, I was tempted to ask if they took reservations. Ranch styled condos lined the drive and a few of the larger units had spacious decks where people lounged at their leisure. I saw a pool and a tennis court to my right all within what looked like a huge sports facility.

I also noticed hardly anyone looked like they were a mere step ahead of the grim reaper and fading fast. Most were vital and a few amazingly energetic people filled the landscape. A couple holding hands crossed my path as I stopped in front of the administration building. It made me feel good to see them still living life, rather than being ushered speedily out of the way. Getting old didn't seem so bad when you watched people like that.

As I exited the rental car, I glanced at my cellphone. Still no signal. I tossed it in the glovebox, clicked the lock on the key fob, and walked into the spacious lobby of the administration building.

"Hello, can I help you?" an older Black man greeted me.

"I'm looking for a Charles Coleman. Cappie," I said.

A smile crept its way across his brown lips and his eyebrows shifted, forcing the lines in his forehead to bunch up like fresh-folded linen. He reached out and took my hand and held it with a strength I would have thought he'd lost long ago. He had the eyes of a man who had gained wisdom from long nights, shattered dreams, and broken promises. But behind them beat the heart of a young boy not quite tired of his playground, not quite done with his game.

"You must be Eddie Gideon, am I right?" he smiled.

"You know me?" I was taken aback.

"I got pictures of you and my granddaughter," he smiled.

"Cappie?" I began to notice the resemblance to Carole in his smile.

"I'm glad to finally meet you son. I hope you brought that sweet granddaughter of mine along with you," he chuckled. "Where is she anyway? Got some surprise planned or something?"

I could feel my mouth go numb and I suddenly couldn't recall a single one of those things I was supposed to remember. My mind went blank. I didn't know what to say at first. Have a seat? Can I get you some coffee?

Nothing. He kept looking at me, like I could have been his long-lost grandson, finally meeting him for the first time, except I had come to break his heart.

"Cappie, I'm sorry. I don't know how to tell you this." I paused and drew a deep breath. "Your granddaughter...she's dead."

I wasn't sure what to expect next, so I held onto his hand. He stared thoughtfully at me for a moment and then he slipped his hand away and walked from the desk and sat down on a sofa near the doors. For a while I didn't move. I just watched him deal with the news, wondering to myself how long it might take the paramedics to get here if I needed them.

This man, who seemed so full of life just moments ago, withered like the most delicate flower before me. Hearing myself say it shocked me almost as much as Cappie. It hit like some stroke of finality, admitting she was dead, affirming it to myself and everyone around me. The thought made me heady and at last I joined Cappie on the sofa.

"She was an only child," he groaned. "She was most beautiful little girl in the world. How could she be dead?"

I didn't think the details mattered right now. There was no need to burden him with the ugliness of what had happened anyway. I sat with my hands folded in my lap and waited for something to come to me that might help him now. What the hell did I know about trying to comfort someone?

In my line of work, we're the guys who deliver the bad news, but even then it's always expected. That's why people hire private investigators, to bring home the unwelcome news, deliver the unbelievable, provide the proof of their suspicions. Priests and ministers were good at this death thing, they knew the right words, it's part of their job. My job had always been to tell people the last thing they wanted to hear, and especially now, the last thing I wanted to say.

"Is there anything I can do?" I spoke to him quietly.

He reached over and squeezed my hand. "Thank you son, this must be just as terrible for you as it is for me."

"Her death came as something of a shock to me." I told the truth for once.

"What kind of world are we livin' in? We're not supposed to out-live our children, let alone our grandchildren. That just ain't right." He wiped his eyes. "This is so hard."

"Would you like me to call someone?"

"There is no one." He tried to smile. "No other relatives left alive but the two of us and now there's just me. Poor girl, struck down in her prime." He reached into his pocket and pulled out an old photo and held it before me.

"This was us in the Virgin Islands two years ago. She loved it there. She always said we'd go back again someday."

"I never knew Carole used to have curly hair," I smiled. "In all the pictures I've seen of her, it was different."

His face changed suddenly, a wary and troubling look crossed his eyes, confusing me some. He sat upright, the photo trembling in his hand. Had I said something to upset him?

"My granddaughter's hair's always been that way, like her mother's hair." He stared at me.

"She'd changed it I guess. Carole's hair was straight. I thought you knew." I needed an exit to this line of conversation.

He looked at the photo again and then squinted back at me. Then he held up the picture again.

"This girl, my granddaughter, is the woman you're talking about?"

"Of course, Cappie, I don't understand—"

"—My granddaughter came to see me three weeks ago, and her hair was not straight." His voice came strong and even. "And my grand-daughter's name is not Carole. It's Jesse. Jesse Coleman."

And the day had just begun.

THIRTEEN

Cappie had just hit me with a gut punch. It was hard not to feel like someone had just floored me as we walked down the road to his place. Cappie had a cozy little apartment with salmon-colored walls and a view of yet another pool off to the right. The large, open concept space served as kitchen, living and dining rooms all in one. The two bedrooms at each end of the apartment opened to a spacious deck with a jacuzzi. I could only dream of living this good.

Cappie made us coffee that had as much bite to it as his revelation about Carole, but I had two stinging cups anyway. So who had I been with all this time? I felt like I had been dining deliciously on calamari without realizing it was really squid. The coffee helped with my ever-uneasy stomach but did nothing for the shock of what I still couldn't quite believe.

"Sure you don't need another?" Cappie held up the pot as I sat at a small square table. "Hate to see half a pot go to waste."

Against my better judgment I let him fill my cup again and then waited for him to sit with me. He seemed to be taking his news a bit better than I was. Perhaps he had resigned himself to this death thing long ago, when friends fell from life faster than he could muster the tears to cry for them. But he had loved this girl from her first moments, when she was small enough to sleep in the crook of his arm. This was his granddaughter, the gleam in his wise, old eyes. And I had to wonder whether or not he was just putting up a front for my benefit.

"I just don't get it, why would she use another name?" I asked. "What could have been her reason?"

"I'm afraid only she and God know the answer to that one, son." He drew down slowly on his cup. "Whatever the reason, it was obviously important enough for her to keep it from us both."

"Could she have been trying to keep someone from finding her? An enemy or an ex-boyfriend?"

He lifted his head and smiled warmly. "She was such a sweet girl. I don't think she had an enemy in the world. And from the looks of it, she landed herself a real fine fella."

It came again, that feeling like this could have been the grandfather I never knew. A gentle, kind man who would give you firecrackers after your mom said no way. I couldn't help but wonder how things might have been had we met a few weeks earlier. Maybe he'd have taken me fishing or to some cheap bar where we'd have gotten thrown out on our ears.

"Did she go peacefully?" he asked.

I'm not sure what it was about his question that made me remember the picture I had taken from Carole's apartment. The same picture I'd been carrying around with me for the last few days hoping to find some insight into all of this. I offered it to Cappie in lieu of the answer I didn't want to utter.

"I remember this," he nodded thoughtfully. "The day after she got that job with that company in Chicago. She was so happy. I'm surprised she gave this to you."

"It was among her things," I said weakly. "I thought that maybe I could..."

"No need to explain." He handed the picture back to me. "You go on and keep it. Jesse would have wanted you to."

"You have to forgive me. I'm having a tough time adjusting to the name change," I smiled. I noticed the hour and realized I didn't have much time left. "Cappie, I really can't stay long. Is there anything I can do for you before I have to leave?"

"Just being here right now has done more for me than you can know, son." He shook my hand firmly. "I'm glad she was with you when her time came."

I made sure Cappie had my address and number to contact me if he ever felt the need to. My own father and I had never been openly affectionate with one another. I never knew him past his emotional walls, and by the time I accepted my adopted father, I had grown too awkward for that sort of thing, too machismo. So I didn't quite know how to handle it when Cappie hugged me. I don't think I ever hugged another man in my life. The experience left me wondering if I had missed out on a few things growing up in a home where men didn't show emotions. I still wasn't sure what to make of the fact that the woman I'd been seeing for the last few months had another name. Again, I questioned how much I knew about this woman.

First, I had to come to terms with the fact that Carole was Jesse. I'd flip a coin on which one of them I slept with later. It was nearly noon and I still had enough time to stop by Mackie's and see Bernice about another burger before I had to be on the plane back home. I prayed the guard at the gate hadn't beat me there.

As soon as I parked the rental car in the airport lot, my cellphone magically connected to a signal again. Between check-in, security, and boarding, I didn't have time to check my voicemails. It was just as well, I needed some time to sort through everything I just learned.

***

All the way back home I thought of only one thing: who knew Carole was really Jesse Coleman? It seemed obvious she had been using the alias since she started working with Prentiss. So who knew she wasn't Carole? Her killer could have, maybe even Derek. There was also the chance that the killer and Derek were one and the same. I wanted to pursue that line, but not too quickly, since I wasn't extremely objective where Derek was concerned anyway.

My cab driver was chatty, so I waited until I was home to listen to my voicemails. The first message came from Kelly, the receptionist I met at Prentiss.

"I need to speak with you sometime today. Please call me as soon as you can." I had to listen twice because her voice was hardly more than a whisper.

I scribbled down both her home and work numbers. The parting look she gave me as I was hauled out of Prentiss didn't inspire any confidence that I'd be speaking with her again. I wondered about that for a moment and then listened to the rest of my messages.

Dr. Kamen's office had left another four messages since yesterday. Unnerving, but whatever it was, it would have to wait.

Why would Kelly be calling me? I wondered if she knew Carole's true identity. I sat at my desk adding to my notes on everything I had discovered over the past few days. When I finished, I sat back and looked at the notes like a four-piece jigsaw puzzle with three pieces missing. Carole or Jesse had a secret, a problem in her life that forced her to become someone else. I knew it had something to do with her murder.

My phone buzzed with a familiar number.

"Hey Lou."

"Gitz, can you come down to the station?"

"Sure, what's up?"

"Just get down here right away." I could hear him shuffling the phone from one ear to the other. "The D.A. was just here, cocky as ever. I get the feeling that they've got something. They might be getting ready to come down on you."

"With what?"

He sighed. "Look, I don't know what they're up to, but they're up to something. That McCrae woman was here yesterday asking about your jacket. She seemed pretty keyed up. Now we can sit here and debate the issue, or you can get your butt down here so we can figure out what's going on."

I didn't waste time asking Lou a lot of questions. I grabbed Kelly's number and stuffed it in my pocket as I slipped down to Deacon's. I hadn't had a chance to touch base with John since I got back from Illinois. When I got down into the bar, Lou wasn't the only one looking for me.

"Like I told you before, he's not here." The tone of John's voice sounded slightly more stern than usual. A telltale sign that you've got maybe two or three more opportunities to get out of his face before he would get nasty with you. It didn't take a genius to figure out that the two officers with Jordan McCrae were looking for me. It looked like I was going to see Lou whether he had called or not. Jordan waved what looked like a summons in John's face which is not the right thing to do when John's angry.

John Deacon had once been a cop like me. One day he found himself on the receiving end of a small fortune some distant relative had left him. John turned his good luck into a solid business. He deserved to live on the finer side of life. Growing up in the ghettos of Cleveland hadn't been kind to him. Even when John became a cop, things still didn't quite go smoothly for him. Most of the home boys he ran with now ran from him. Close friends became bitter enemies. But John was tough enough to deal with the flack, even when it came from his own family. One night he got caught up in a shootout between a couple of rival gangs. A former friend decided not to let John take him in. John had to shoot him. After that, nothing was quite the same. He moved to Columbus a month later. John and I had that in common—two men despised for doing the job we loved most in life.

"Excuse me." I cut into their bickering. "Somebody here looking for me?"

"Mr. Gideon." Jordan turned to me and smiled. "You didn't answer your door."

"You must've knocked while I was in the shower," I lied.

"Well, I'm glad you didn't leave town. I would have hated to have to go to the trouble of getting a warrant for your arrest." She sauntered toward me. Her legs looked just as stunning in motion as they had sitting bar-side. She handed me the summons, then folded her arms in front of her.

"All this way just to bring me a present?" I smiled.

"You almost sound as smug as Nelson." She gave me a curious look. "Did the two of you play in the same sandbox or something?"

"I think you'll find there isn't too much of anything Nelson and I have in common," I replied.

"Outside of the fact you hate each other." Her eyes lit up with a sudden fascination. "What is it that makes you two mortal enemies, Mr. Gideon? What makes two men hate each other so much?"

"I don't think you have that much time," I glanced over the summons. "Tomorrow morning? You must really be as good as Nelson thinks you are."

"Around the courthouse, I've been called Crazy Legs McCrae." She said with a very wicked grin. "I don't believe in wasting the taxpayers' money or my own time. And you're avoiding my question."

"You mean Nelson and me?" I laughed. "Sure, maybe over dinner one night this week."

"How about tonight? I know a great grilled chicken and seafood place on the west side." She said it with a straight face.

"You're crazy," I stammered. "Aside from the fact that you just handed me a summons and I'm the prime suspect in the case you're currently assigned to, Nelson would have your hide for even thinking about that."

Her hands shifted to her hips. "Nelson may be my boss, but he doesn't own me. What I do on my own time is my business. I don't depend on him to carry my caseload or have him hold my hand when I can't get a deposition back on time, and I don't cry when I break a nail."

"Is this a little payback from the first night we met? Or is this a sample of your fiery Irish temper?" I asked.

Someone once told me that a woman who couldn't blush was a woman you couldn't trust. From the color on her face and the smile curling out of the corner of her mouth, Jordan could be well worth trusting.

We sat down at a corner table and for the third time today, I had coffee. She pointed the two officers toward the door and they walked over and posted themselves there. I got the feeling Jordan was used to playing hardball with men, more so in the workplace than anywhere else.

"I don't want you to take this the wrong way," I held up my hands. "But talking with me like this can compromise things for you and I'd hate to see that happen."

Her delightful grin returned. "You sound as though you want me to win this case."

"I want you to get the person who killed Carole."

"And obviously that person isn't you?" She leaned back in her chair. "According to a Derek Simmons, you had a reason to kill her. Off the record of course."

"What on earth would make him believe I had anything to do with her murder?"

"Why wouldn't he?" she snapped back.

"Not even the police would be stupid enough to let it slip. Up until the other day he didn't even know me," I thought aloud. "Off the record, Derek Simmons may have had reasons of his own for wanting her dead."

"Would you care to share any of those alleged reasons?"

"Let's just say that I'm still at the evidence gathering stage. I don't want to say anything until I can be sure of what I suspect," I smiled. "I may need some of this when I see you in court."

She sighed. "You'll need more than a hunch, Mr. Gideon. Even if you're telling the truth, you were still found at the murder scene with the victim."

I sipped my coffee. "Call me Gitz."

She looked me over with a quick glance, scanning my face for some sign that might give her an inkling of what I had up my sleeve. She finished her coffee, stood, and waved at the two officers. "I'm ready, guys."

"Leaving so soon?" I asked.

"It's almost five and I still have a few leads of my own to run down before we get together tomorrow," she smiled.

"In that case would you do me one small favor?"

"Try me." She leaned against the table.

"Whatever happens, promise we'll still do that dinner."

She tilted her head at first, puzzled by my words. Then she nodded, shrugged her shoulders and she left with the officers.

I didn't feel good about the surprise I planned to slam her with in court, but I didn't have much choice. And if I was going to pull it off, I needed to get back to the coroner's office. Skip might be able to confirm some things. Then I planned to find Derek Simmons.

"Hey, Gitz," John called out, holding up my cell. "Phone's buzzing."

I figured it must have been Lou worried sick about what Jordan and Nelson were up to. I thought of making up some corny story that would make him choke, but it wasn't Lou.

"Eddie, its Doctor Kamen," his voice sounded harried. "I need you to come to the clinic today."

"Sure. What's up?"

He paused. "Well, your blood tests came back and I need to treat you right away."

I paused. "Treat me for what?"

"Eddie, I think you may have been poisoned."

FOURTEEN

Thursday morning Jordan and her entourage were already dug in by the time I arrived at the courthouse with my attorney, Melvin Greene. She looked up at me between briefs and then quickly returned to ironing out the details of her approach with her assistants. Lolita Cain, the presiding judge, was a stern looking woman with a face as solid as her commitment to the justice system. I had only appeared before her once before, when Nelson somehow slipped and fell on my fist.

"Alright ladies and gentlemen," she pushed her glasses up on her nose. "I've got a full docket today and I'm not really fond of having to juggle my schedule for a prelim."

"We appreciate the court's indulgence on this matter, Your Honor," Jordan addressed the judge. "And we'll try to—"

"—Ms. McCrae, before you think about offering me any apologies, don't. Mr. Gideon, I'm glad to see you've retained legal counsel this time." Unfortunately, she remembered our last meeting.

"Melvin Greene, Your Honor. And we're ready to begin at once." Mel wasn't one to mince words. He was the best lawyer money could buy, at least my money anyway. His fee always stayed the same: my season tickets to the OSU basketball games.

"Then let's proceed." The judge leaned back in her chair.

"Thank you, Your Honor." Jordan stepped forward. "Your Honor, on the night of August 14, a young woman, Carole Spenser of 2285 Willow Court, was murdered in cold blood. The following morning, police acting on an anonymous tip, found Mr. Gideon in bed with the deceased after he murdered her."

"Objection, Your Honor!" Melvin raised his voice. "Circumstantial. Counsel hasn't proven that my client killed anyone."

"Ms. McCrae, this is only a preliminary hearing, I suggest we keep the dramatics to a minimum and stick to facts," the judge advised. "I'll hear opening remarks from the defendant's counsel now."

"But Your Honor I—"

"—I said I'll hear defendant's counsel now, Ms. McCrae, or do you have an objection?" Judge Cain really had her dander up for some reason today.

"This is highly out of order, Judge Cain," Jordan replied.

"So was going to the Court Administrator to rearrange my docket to have your case moved to the head of the line, Ms. McCrae. Seeing as how I have been inconvenienced, I think I'm entitled to run my courtroom as I see fit."

You could almost hear Jordan's fists as they clenched.

"As you wish, Your Honor." The anguish in her voice was subtle.

Mel opened his files and pulled several sheets out to begin his summation.

"Your Honor, my client was indeed found in bed, lying next to the body of woman, who several hours before had been murdered. But beyond that, the prosecutor has no real evidence that my client was involved in any wrongdoing. The medical examiner's report shows that the deceased's neck was broken and she was shot in the chest. There was no gun found at the scene. My client's hands bore no powder marks, burns, or blood. No indication that he had tried to wash any such substance away. In fact, the only blood forensics found was on the victim and her side of the bed. No spatter, and not a drop on my client. He did not attempt to flee the scene. When police arrived in response to the anonymous call, he was found soundly sleeping and appeared surprised. My client's only crime is being in the wrong place at the wrong time." Melvin moved back and forth between the tables. "More to the point, Your Honor, the prosecution's case is at best flimsy and at worst a witch-hunt against a former police officer."

"Objection!" Jordan stood.

"Ms. McRae—" the judge began to rule.

"—Your Honor, the prosecution contends that my client willfully murdered Carole Spenser, when in fact they are not even sure themselves who has been murdered!"

"Your Honor, I object!!" Jordan called out again. "And you haven't ruled on my previous objection to the witch hunt accusation."

"Mr. Greene, can you back up your claim or—"

"—Your Honor, if you please, I believe we can bring this matter to an end in thirty seconds." Melvin pointed to the clock on the wall.

"Overruled, but for your sake Mr. Greene, you'd better," the judge warned.

"The prosecution claims that my client killed Carole Spenser. If this is their case, then where is Carole Spenser?" Melvin said.

"I beg your pardon?" Jordan stuttered.

"So do I. Explain yourself, Mr. Greene," the judge leaned forward.

"My client could not have killed Carole Spenser because there is no Carole Spenser." Melvin offered the sheets he held to both the judge and Jordan. "This is the coroner's report which includes fingerprints and dental records sent to us via the victim's grandfather in Illinois. Both records clearly show that the deceased was not Carole Spenser."

"Your Honor, I strongly object to this!" Jordan fired back. "The contents of these documents should have been made available to my office in discovery."

Melvin held more documents up before the judge. "These materials were just faxed to my office this morning Your Honor, along with a blood test report by Dr. Nick Kamen which is extremely relevant to this case."

"Relevant in what way?" Judge Cain asked.

"Dr. Kamen's examination revealed that my client was drugged on the night in question." Melvin handed a copy to Jordan. "When Mr. Gideon called me yesterday from his doctor's office, I was first concerned with his mental state. But after speaking with his doctor and then receiving this report, it was clear my client has been the victim of foul play. Mr. Gideon is suffering from toxic poisoning, brought on by exposure to trichloromethane, commonly known as chloroform."

Melvin moved to the bench to give Judge Cain a copy of the documents. "Both were found in my client's blood test, and the coroner obtained a sample of chloroform from a pillow at the crime scene."

"Your Honor, this is completely out of order," Jordan protested. "No such evidence was ever brought to my attention."

"And how convenient for your case that they weren't!" Melvin turned to Jordan. "How many times has the District Attorney's office wasted taxpayer dollars trying to frame my client on whatever charges they could throw together?"

"Mr. Greene!"

"To what lengths is the District Attorney's office willing to go to in order to pursue their own self-interests? How long will the D.A. blame my client for his father's death?!"

"Mr. Greene, that will be quite enough!!" Judge Cain banged her gavel, "One more outburst like that and I'll hold you in contempt. I don't know what the hell is going on here! Counselors—in my chambers, now!"

I wasn't sure whether to sit or stand. I hadn't expected this little revelation would cause such a stir. Hell, I did. I knew what would happen. Jordan's face was drained of color. The shock of what Melvin implied meant that she had become the very thing she despised, worse yet, she had been used. She knew now why she had been assigned to this case and why Nelson himself didn't have the balls to face me in court. I had dreaded this moment for her. In a way, I had used her too. Maybe she was right after all about Nelson and I having something in common.

Fifteen minutes later, it was all over. Melvin convinced the judge to dismiss the charges in exchange for my full cooperation with the D.A.'s office on the murder of Jesse Coleman. When they returned from the judge's chambers, Jordan's face was a mixture of anger and disbelief, both directed at me. I couldn't blame her for the way she felt, but I had to make her understand why I kept what I knew from her.

I grabbed her arm as she strode past me in the corridor. "Jordan, I want to say I'm sorry and—"

From the way she slapped me across the face I knew she wasn't ready to see things from my point of view.

"Counselor! What are y—" Melvin stepped in, but I stopped him.

She deserved to air her grievances against me.

"—Y'know, yesterday I thought that maybe somewhere beneath all that macho bullshit was a decent guy." She gritted her teeth. "Now I know there's only more bullshit."

"I suppose I deserve that," I said sheepishly.

"That and a whole lot more. You and Nelson just made me the laughingstock of the county."

"This wasn't personal, Jordan," I tried to project sincerity.

"Really? Tell me something. How many other casualties are you and Nelson responsible for, Mr. Gideon? How many other people have you used in this stupid game the two of you play?"

"That's not fair, Jordan," I whispered.

"Like you said, I guess we both made a mistake, didn't we?"

"Jordan. I'm really sorry."

"Go to hell," she hissed.

As I watched her leave the courthouse, I wondered how long it would be before my past stopped interfering with my future. Had I known back then the trouble doing the right thing would cause now, would I have opened my mouth? Would I have done what my partner told me to do and looked the other way? If I had, would I still have my badge? How different would my life have been? Boy, did I need a beer.

***

Disillusioned as I felt with myself, I still managed to return Kelly's call. We arranged to meet for dinner at a place on the north end called The Oyster Dock. She sounded anxious on the phone but wouldn't discuss anything, which only made me more eager to hear what she had to say later. As I was hanging up with her, I noticed a new voicemail notification. I tapped it and was surprised to hear the message. Cappie.

"I've been giving the matter of why Jesse changed her name some thought, and I think you're right that she may have been trying to keep someone from finding her," he said. "I remembered a few things about a young man she dated in college. Jesse graduated from the University of Illinois back in '11. Call me soon."

I hadn't considered Cappie might be able to provide a lead on why Jesse had a reason to use a phony name. I scribbled down the number he left for the university and the year Jesse graduated. I also wrote down what Kelly had told me about Carole coming from their corporate office in Chicago and an explosion went off in my head. If the idea that I had brewing was right, then I had more than one reason to want to punch Derek Simmons in the mouth.

At home, I took some time to crunch the information I had gathered while I mellowed out to a little Benny Mardones in the background. As I glossed over all my notes, I wondered what Derek could have done to make Jesse feel she had to hide who she really was? What was he capable of? If it wasn't him, then who or what frightened her into living life as someone else? Though a part of me wanted to just pound the answers out of him, I knew I had to be craftier than that. Derek was used to cutting deals in the corporate world. High-level trading wasn't enough for him. Money seemed to be the first and last word with Derek. Maybe because of it he killed Jesse and forced her to become Carole.

***

I found Kelly waiting for me outside of The Oyster Dock. Being prompt must have been one of her assets to Prentiss, right on time at 8:15. Kelly wore a red dress that hugged her mid-thigh. She had done something with her hair. Tight, cute little curls brushed against her cheeks. For a beautiful woman, Kelly looked more like a scared child.

"I'm so glad you got here," she sighed in relief. "Let's go inside, I don't feel safe out here."

"Kelly, are you alright?" I reached for her hand. It felt cold against mine.

"I'm fine now." She drew a deep breath and I held the door for her.

Kelly called over the maître d' and we hurried to our table. She ordered us a bottle of wine and a tray of oysters. I had to wonder from her selections what her intentions toward me were. Was this the same sweet girl I had met a few days ago? Or was she here for something else?

"I'm sorry. I'm not usually like this." She wrenched her hands until her knuckles were bone white.

"Why don't you take a minute to gather yourself." I wrapped my hands over hers. "You seem a little tense."

She reached for her glass of wine, quickly swallowing every drop.

"What I have to tell you is profoundly serious. It could mean my job if anyone sees me here. Do you think we were followed?"

I gave her a warm smile. "Kelly, we're all alone. No one knows we're meeting. It's okay. Why don't you tell me what's on and then we can relax?"

"I'm acting paranoid, aren't I?" she managed to smile.

"You said you had something to tell me."

"I'm not sure where to start. I felt really bad after what happened with you and Derek. I just couldn't believe it when he told me that you had something to do with Carole's murder." She took another sip of wine. "I thought my day couldn't get any worse until they showed up."

"They who?" I asked.

"Some guys from the Securities Exchange Commission and the I.R.S.," she replied. "They wanted to talk to Carole. They had warrants and some other official looking documents. They had everybody scared out of their minds."

"Why would a visit from the S.E.C. scare everyone?"

"I don't know, but usually it means that someone has been doing something illegal." She took another sip of wine.

"So what did they want with Carole?" I asked.

"They wanted access to all her client files. Anything she had worked on in the last six months. Something about some discrepancies in a few of her transactions. The I.R.S. called Stock Watch."

"What's Stock Watch?" I asked.

"Watchdogs of the industry." She stabbed at an oyster with her fork. "They monitor who's buying large blocks of stock, things like that."

"What kind of discrepancies were they looking for?" I inquired.

"I didn't catch all of what they said, but I heard someone mention that a large cash figure was involved."

"How large a figure?"

"Ten million, maybe more." Her eyes searched the room for anyone who might be eavesdropping. "This is all so terrible, and right after Carole was murdered."

I began to wonder just how terrible. Ten million dollars made quite a motive for someone to commit murder. Definitely the right price if you could walk away with that much in cash, no taxes and no one to trace it back to you. This was all starting to get a little strange. Carole gets murdered, then Carole isn't Carole, now the S.E.C and the I.R.S. believe she was involved in some illegal ten mill deal?

"Kelly, tell me what's got you so upset." I put the question to her. "Does the I.R.S. think you're involved in this somehow?"

"Oh my god, no!" she gasped. Then she looked around the restaurant again, as if she hoped to find someone staring at us. Why? What had her freaked out?

"It was Derek. I've never seen anyone so angry before in my life." Her hands shook.

I took her hand. "What was he so angry about?"

"It was strange actually. A certified check was delivered to the office for Derek the other day. When he saw it, he went crazy. He grabbed me and demanded to know who told me to give it to him. I tried to explain that it came by certified mail, but he was in such a frenzy, I thought he could be dangerous." I saw fear fill her eyes. "I thought he might hurt me."

"Why didn't you call the police?" I asked. "Did you report what happened to his boss?"

"I was going to, but he came back a few minutes later and apologized for being such a total jerk. He scared me so much before that I just decided to let it go at that," she sighed.

"Kelly, I have to ask you this. After everything Derek must have said about me, why did want you to meet with me?"

She shrugged slightly. "I can't say really, I just felt like I could trust you. I think if Carole were alive, she'd tell me to trust you."

I brought my hands to my face to conceal the pain in my eyes. Kelly brought my feelings for Carole to the surface. I found myself feeling a closeness to the woman sitting in front of me. A shared trauma.

"I still don't get why he'd go off about getting a check?" I wondered aloud.

"Neither did I at first. But then later when I went to take Derek some documents to sign, I overheard him talking with someone on the phone. He was still angry about getting the check. He said something about it being stupid to do that, something about it being dangerous for everyone." She took a deep breath and drew her hands over her face. "I didn't hear much after that. He turned around and I handed him the forms. I was just thankful to be away from him."

"Who was the check from?"

"That was the strange part. I recognized the name from one of the accounts. But I'm sure she wasn't one of Derek's clients," she said.

"Who's client was it then?"

"I don't recall, but her name was Jesse Coleman."

"Excuse me, Miss?" The damned waiter had lousy timing. "This note was left for you."

I looked at Kelly. "I thought you said no one knew we were meeting."

"Just my boyfriend." She looked sheepish. "He dropped me off earlier. Will you excuse me a minute?"

I nodded as I began to ponder just how deep all of this was getting. There wasn't any doubt in my mind about Derek being involved now. No doubt that he was in the apartment with us the night Carole died. If he hadn't forced her to become Carole, maybe he extorted her into getting involved in whatever I.R.S. mess she was in. But why couldn't Carole have come to me with the truth and who else was involved? Derek must have had an accomplice. That would explain him getting crazy over the check from Jesse's account. Derek must have been shitting his pants when the S.E.C. people came to seize Carole's files.

Then the rumbling in my gut came back on me, like I'd had too much coffee again. Except this time, it wasn't from the poison or any drug I'd been given. Something felt wrong.

I picked up the note the waiter brought to Kelly.

Meet me outside. –Nick

Why outside, why not come in and walk her out?

I told the waiter to box up the oysters and headed for the entrance. Out of instinct I reached inside my jacket and popped the safety on my gun. It had started raining, so I paused just inside the door to turn my jacket collar up. I caught sight of Kelly standing in the middle of the parking lot, glancing around. Maybe I was wrong, maybe my nerves were just edgy from all the medication I'd had to take.

Suddenly the headlights from an oncoming car caught my attention. It was moving too fast. The tires screeched as the car cut across the lot and headed in Kelly's direction.

"Kelly!" I screamed, bursting through the doors with my gun drawn.

She turned just seconds before the car was upon her, but seconds weren't enough. Kelly slammed hard against the hood. The sound of flesh hitting steel making a horrid noise as she cried out. Her body rolled over the top of the car. Then her cries stopped abruptly as she fell into a heap on the wet pavement.

"Hey!" I ran after it. "Son of a bitch didn't even try to stop! He meant to kill her!"

I chased the car out of the lot toward the highway. I squeezed off six or seven rounds but the only thing I managed to do was blow out the back window before he floored it up the on-ramp. I couldn't stop him. The bastard got away.

"Kelly!" I ran back into the parking lot. "Kelly!"

Several waitstaff and restaurant patrons were already gawking helplessly around her.

"Back up. Move it! Don't touch her!" I pushed my way through and knelt beside her. "Has anyone called an ambulance?!"

"On its way," someone muttered.

As bad as she took it, Kelly wasn't dead. Her pulse was weak and her breathing was shallow. Her head and face were full of blood and bruises.

"Kelly." I kept my voice low. I yanked my jacket off and knelt down to stabilize her head and neck with my knees. "Don't worry Kelly. The ambulance will be here in a sec. Just hold on, sweetheart."

I wanted to wipe away the gravel imbedded in her cheek but I knew it would only cause her more pain. Her right leg was twisted unnaturally just below the knee, undoubtedly broken. A pool of blood was spreading on the ground from beneath her torso. She tried to squeeze my hand but her strength wasn't there. Her breath was quick and clipped, probably from multiple broken ribs.

"I... I'm... c-cold." She managed between gasps.

Careful not to jostle her neck, I draped my jacket over her. I tried to make her as comfortable as I could. Damn, where was that ambulance?

"Hold on Kelly, you're gonna make it."

"I'm so cold," she said.

"Just stay with me, Kelly," I pulled the jacket up to her chin. "Stay with me now. You're gonna make it."

Kelly's hand suddenly slipped between my fingers. Her breathing halted.

Instinctively, my emergency training took over. I waved a waiter over to take my place.

"Keep her neck still," I heard myself demand, as I started chest compressions.

She had to make it. She had to be alright. I was desperate to get her breathing again. I covered her nose and blew into her mouth. Nothing. I did more compressions. More puffs. No pulse. No breath. The ambulance roared into the lot, splashing through a small pothole. The small crowd parted and the EMTs stepped in, but I knew it was too late. She lay still and silent, just like the body in the morgue, just like Carole. Dammit, she was just a fuckin' kid. Kelly was dead. The sky opened up and the drizzle became a downpour. Another woman who trusted me to protect her had died. As they worked methodically on her lifeless body I stepped out of the way. There, in the cold, steady rain, I could only feel one thing. Rage. I was seriously pissed.

FIFTEEN

This was one of those moments in life so staggeringly jarring that everything feels like it's sped up and in slow motion at the same time. The kind where all of one's senses experience the event, all at once. Kelly's body being tossed up over the car and onto the pavement. My gun shattering the perp's back window. The flashing emergency lights and the flash of the ME's camera. Yellow tape being stretched across the crime scene. The cold rain soaking through my shirt. Sticky, warm blood stains on my pants. Kelly's boyfriend Nick sobbing as the police gave him the news. The smallest details become forever part of the fabric of the memory. I have too many of these types of memories.

Nick gave me a burning look as they escorted him to a waiting squad car. He had every right to blame me for Kelly's death. I should've known better than to let her walk out of the restaurant alone. She feared someone might be after her but I didn't take her seriously.

I just finished giving make, model, and part of the license plate to a uniform when Lou slid up beside me, digging into a pack of cigarettes.

"Partial plate? This is a real mess, Gitz. What the hell are you involved in?"

"She was a friend Lou. Somebody who was trying to help."

"Your friend just bought herself a ride to the morgue, Gitz. I'd hate to see you take the same ride." The rain made it hard for him to get a light. He motioned to the overhang above the restaurant entrance. "Talk to me over there."

We stepped over and he lit up as I started talking. "It was Derek Simmons."

"Can you prove that you saw him?" he pursed his lips, exhaling.

"Yeah, he fuckin' jumped out of the car and shook my hand all right?!" I fumed. "What the hell are we standing here for?! How come you don't have somebody shakin' his tree? Better still, let me do it for you!"

Lou flicked the ash off his cigarette. "Let's get one goddamned thing straight, Gitz. You try to go off and play cowboy and I'll stick your ass in a hole and forget your name! If you want to help, go give the officer a statement and take your Black ass home!"

I threw my hands up. "That girl came here tonight to help me. Kelly had information about this case. She came to me looking for help and got killed for it!"

He tossed his cigarette on the ground and stuck his finger in my chest. "Which don't earn you dick! You may walk the walk but you don't wear a shield anymore. You are one damn fine P.I. but that doesn't mean a fucking thing to that girl lying over there." He pointed to where Nick stood moments earlier. "The only guy with a right to fly off the handle right now is trying to figure out how to tell her family she's dead."

"Lou, I—"

"—I know you're hurting and I don't envy you that. But if you don't stop going off halfcocked, more people could end up dead. Maybe even be you."

"I can handle this," I said.

"Bullshit!" he snapped. "Eddie, you had the makings of a good cop—you still do. But you didn't learn everything about being a cop. What it means to suck it up and remember that we go by the letter of the law even when the law stinks. You think I do this crap because I like being out here in the damned rain? I do it because I believe in something. Just like I believed in you."

As much as I hated to admit it, Lou's sermon brought me back down to earth. He made me remember when I first got my badge and nobody wanted to be bothered with me, except a hard-nosed sergeant, who saw a little of himself in this green rookie.

"Lou, when I came out with the truth about Petey, how come you stood by me?"

"Petey was a good friend." He dug for another cigarette. "But he was a lousy cop and didn't deserve to wear the uniform." He lit the cigarette and took a quick puff. "You ever wonder why when we pull up in some neighborhoods and people get nervous—they don't trust us? It's because of guys like Nelson Peters. He made things bad for us. A lot of cops were pissed over what you did. Some still are."

"What else is new?" I sighed.

"But there were some of us back then, a handful of us who believed in what you did and were proud of you. Sometimes you have to risk everything to do what's right. Even if you have to take down someone you care about. You don't ask why. You just do it 'cause it's right." He drew on the smoldering cigarette.

"So how do I know if it was all worth it?"

"That ain't for me to answer, Gitz. The bottom line is you made a choice and you're the only one who has to live with it." He puffed again. "Go home, Gitz. Just go home."

Lou walked back to the squad car and I slowly walked toward my car. I gnawed on Lou's speech all the way home and long into the night. But even after 120 sit-ups, 45 minutes on the bike, and a hot shower, I still felt just as keyed up as when I walked in the door. It was close to three a.m. and I wasn't even close to feeling drowsy. Kelly's death played over and over in my mind like an old record with a scratch in the middle. The image of her body flailing against the car hit like a nail being driven further and further into my mind, as if to permanently mark the event. I didn't want to sit at home and do nothing. Not with a murderer on the loose.

I parked my car just outside of Carole's complex. I waited a good thirty minutes after the last of her neighbors' lights went out, praying they were snug in their beds. I crept up to her front door, lock pick in hand, and knelt down in the darkness. A small-time hood I busted once taught me how to use this thing. Considering the number of times I've locked myself out of my own place, I haven't regretted it. Normally I could pick a decent lock in a little under a minute, but tonight I didn't feel the need to rush.

Ten minutes later, I crawled into Carole's apartment. The place had lost its fragrant feminine charm to the hands of sweaty police detectives and forensics specialists that trudged through in the last few days. A musky aroma now mixed with the last remnants of her perfume.

I scanned the room as best I could in the dark, trying to focus on something. I knew better than to use the flashlight on my cell—too big. I dug deep in my pockets and yanked out a tiny flashlight and swept the room, before that uneasy feeling crept back over me again.

Carole's voice played like a warped record in my mind. I measured my steps back toward the bedroom where I'd last held her and paused. A wave of grief enveloped me like a straitjacket. I stood there wondering what I might find as my hand raised toward the light switch; ghosts, visions of death, what? This was getting me nowhere. I had to get over my emotions, put this bleeding-heart shit aside and do the one thing I did better than anyone I knew. I hit the switch with an angry thrust. The twin lamps on either side of the bed filled the room with light and my fears retreated into the darkness.

There wasn't much left that the police hadn't thoroughly gone over: the sheets and pillowcase had been taken, the lamps themselves were still marked from where fingerprints had been taken, and the bed was still taped off. I circled the bed first, thinking with each step about everything I'd learned thus far.

Dr. Kamen's discovery about the chloroform had me wondering just how someone could have drugged me without my knowing. It explained the traces they found on the pillowcase. They could have introduced the drug to the pillow and then given me a heavier dose when they came out of hiding. So where did they hide? Was Derek inside with us the whole time?

A noise in the outer room nearly made me drop my flashlight. I switched off the bedroom light and jumped back toward the hallway. Damn, I should have never turned it on in the first place. Maybe one of her neighbors had seen the light from the back. I waited to hear any other sound, nothing. I began to wonder if someone other than a neighbor had followed me inside. I eased my gun out of its holster and slid against the wall back toward the living room. The streetlights from the parking lot threw odd shapes across the room. I paused and weighed what few options I had: either wait for whoever else was inside to find me or find them first. I took two steps into the living room and swung to my right. My ears caught something that made me wish I'd gone left. Two clicks came from behind me. It could have been the sound of the place settling.

But after being shot at a number of times, one could hardly forget the sound of a .38 being cocked.

"One wrong move, and I'll use your head to paint the walls." Her voice sounded softer than usual. "Drop your weapon and turn around slowly." From the look on her face she was even more surprised than I.

"Nice night isn't it, Counselor?" I grinned.

SIXTEEN

I put on a fresh pot of coffee and tried to put something together for us to snack on. After bumping into one another at Carole's, I suggested we come back to my place and compare notes. There wasn't much in the fridge. Half a jar of peanut butter, a couple of grapefruits, a half-eaten muffin, and a chicken breast. I hadn't taken the time to do my usual shopping. I grabbed the fruit and looked to see how Jordan was getting along.

From the way she was dressed, Jordan had done this sort of thing before. Her long red hair stuffed underneath a black knit snow-cap. She wore a dark sweatshirt over a Lycra body suit that wrapped around all the right curves. She gracefully slipped out of her hiking boots and yanked the cap from her head, freeing her billowy red strands.

"How do you like your coffee?" I called out.

"I'm trying to cut back. Just water will be fine," she replied. "So tell me what you were doing at Carole Spenser's apartment—I mean Jesse Coleman's apartment."

I poured a cup of coffee for myself and drew her water, then brought the drinks and sliced fruit in on a serving tray. Seeing her in casual clothes surprised me. I hadn't realized until now just how attractive Jordan looked. Athleisure wear suited her much better than her usual matronly legal attire.

I found it hard to remember she was the woman who wanted to throw me in jail this morning. From her toned form to her smart mouth, Jordan was captivating. She moved over to the piano where she simply studied the keys. I reached for a coaster and placed it on top of some sheet music on the piano.

"Do you play?"

"My mother used to make me take lessons when I was eight," she smiled.

"Never too late to learn." I sat next to her on the bench.

Jordan turned to me slowly, squinting as she tried to decipher what my comment might have meant, rather than just taking it for what it was. She took the glass of water from my hand and brought it to her lips, swallowing it all in the space of seconds. Then she set it down on the coaster and stared at the keys again.

"You want another?" I swallowed hard.

"You ready to talk to me about this murder?"

"What about it?" I sipped my coffee.

She jabbed a red fingernail at me. "You knew about Jesse Coleman before we entered that courtroom. You knew when I gave the summons. You got the case thrown out on a technicality and then you break into the murder victim's apartment. I want to know, why?"

"In case you forgot counselor, you broke in before I did. So before you get all high and mighty, explain to me why an assistant district attorney is risking two to six for Breaking and Entering?"

"To get the person who killed Jesse Coleman," she said.

"So how come we're getting in each other's way instead of working together?" I stroked a few keys.

"Still holding to the opinion that you're innocent?"

I got up and moved over to the sofa. I was tired and annoyed by Jordan's insinuations.

"It's more than an opinion. It's a statement of fact," I said. "Why in the hell are you here if you think I killed her? You found me breaking into her apartment, which must prove something?"

"Not nearly enough, Mr. Gideon."

"Lady, what the hell do you want from me?" I raised my voice. "So you got screwed in court today, big deal. A girl was murdered tonight trying to help me find out who really killed Jesse. Do you think I give a damn that you got spanked in court? I don't owe you jack and given the choice between your career and my ass? You can guess which one I'd choose."

"Hold on. Someone was killed?"

I sat my cup on the floor and went to my window to take in the sunrise. "Her name was Kelly," I sighed heavily.

The smell from the bakery up the street already filled the air with hints blueberry filled croissants and chocolate donuts. The orange haze of the morning lit up the buildings and trees like neon fixtures. I stood there thinking not so much of the beautiful morning or the wondrous light, but of the women who hadn't lived to see it. Carole—Jesse, and poor Kelly. Today would be just another day that most of the world would take for granted with subtle indifference.

"Kelly was a receptionist at Prentiss Securities. Jesse—er, Carole used to work there. Kelly believed she had some information that might have helped me find out who killed Carole."

"What kind of information?"

"Something involving the S.E.C. and the I.R.S. They've seized all of her client files and anything else she was working on. They think Carole wasn't on the up and up about certain transactions she made for a number of clients. Ten million dollars' worth in fact."

"Ten million dollars?" Jordan stammered.

"Quite a motive for murder, don't you think?" I looked back to see the expression on her face. "Kelly also received a certified check from a client. The check was for Derek Simmons."

"So he gets a check. What's so unusual about that?"

"The client was Jesse Coleman."

I imagined the look on Jordan's face matched what Kelly saw in my eyes when she gave me the news about Derek and the check. Jordan leaned on the piano and ran her fingers through her hair. She bit down on her lower lip as her mind sorted through the information. Derek was involved in this somehow.

"How can I get a hold of this Kelly?" her eyes widened.

"Lady, are you thick? Didn't you just hear what I said? Kelly is dead! She walked out of the restaurant and somebody ran her down. She died in my arms!" I snarled.

"Oh right. God, I'm sorry." She turned away from me. "Really, I am truly sorry. I didn't mean to be cruel. I just spaced. I haven't slept well lately."

"Forget it, nothing either of us can do about it anyway."

"Is that why you were at the apartment?" she asked softly.

I went back over to the sofa and leaned back. "I really don't know what I expected to find there. I'm sure Derek knew who Carole really was. I don't think the cops told him who I was but he recognized me from the jump at Prentiss. He may have even been extorting her. Kelly told me that when she gave Derek the check from Jesse he started acting crazy.

Then later she overheard him telling someone it could be dangerous to contact him there."

"An accomplice maybe?" Jordan wondered aloud.

"I thought the same thing. Derek and Carole knew one another in college. Her grandfather told me about a boyfriend she had in college she may have wanted to get away from. My guess is its Derek. They both worked for Prentiss in Chicago."

"So go to the police, tell them your story."

"I can't." I sat upright. "I've got nothing solid to prove that he's the one who killed Carole or Kelly. I'm not even sure how to link him with the chloroform they used on me."

"Right. And the thing with the check could have been done through the normal channels of business. Even the call Kelly heard could be dismissed as hearsay. So now what?"

"I'll go over and beat a confession out of him."

"Oh that'd really be bright," she sighed. "I thought you were smarter than that."

"I'm not in the mood, counselor." I gritted my teeth.

She stared at me. "What are you in the mood for? Murder?"

"Look, I'm no Phi Beta Kappa, but it doesn't take a genius to see that Derek could be the trigger man. I'm startin' to get a little ticked that I'm the only one seeing this. In the last few days I've been booked, beaten, and accused of murdering the woman I loved, so I think I'm entitled to a little attitude right about now."

"So what you really mean is seeking justice is not as satisfying as revenge." She got up and came towards me. "I'd really like to help you get the person who killed these women. For what it's worth I think you may be right about all this. But I won't be party to some vendetta."

Jordan grabbed her things and headed for the door. I wondered if she was right about me wanting revenge more than I wanted justice.

"If you plan to do the right thing, I'll back you any way I can."

She headed for the door and left me to ponder the matter. Maybe it just ticked me off that she knew me better than I was willing to admit. But two wrongs had already been made and not much had happened to make them right. Derek felt like an annoying pimple that I was seething to squeeze the life out of. So maybe the good counselor had a point and I needed to check myself before I did anything else. I eased back on the sofa. Sleep was finally starting to wash over me. I looked forward to the coming weekend.

***

I was only able to sleep for about four hours. I jumped from the couch around 11:30 am and stood in the shower for about twenty minutes. I still couldn't shake what had happened to Kelly last night. Maybe it was good that I didn't. The thought of Kelly gave me the strength to get by despite the lack of sleep.

The first thing I did was put in a call to Cappie. I'd missed him the last time he called and he might feel better knowing that the police weren't sitting on their hands. The phone to his room rang until it went to voicemail. No answer. Then I decided to follow up on what he had told me in his message. I called the University of Illinois alumni records department.

"Marge Barker, may I help you?" She answered in a nasal midwestern accent.

"Yes Marge, my name is Louis Brandon." I lied. "I'm a detective with the police here in Columbus, Ohio. I wondered if you could help me."

"What can we do for you, Mr. Brandon?" Her voice had a warm, musical quality.

"I'm trying to find out about two former students." I reached over and grabbed my notebook. Midway through the page, I'd written Carole and Derek's dates of birth and other pertinent information. "Their names are Carole Spenser and Derek Simmons."

"Is that Spenser with a C or an S?" Marge asked.

In my zeal, I almost forgot that Carole wasn't Carole. "I'm sorry, I meant to say Jesse Coleman and Derek Simmons," I clarified.

"Mm-hmm. And do you have the last four digits of their socials?"

Thankfully I did, and I read them to her.

I could hear her nails striking her keyboard with an accuracy that came from years of typing. She hummed joyously as she waited for the computers to dig up the information she searched for. Whether she hummed for my benefit or her own I couldn't tell, the sound of her voice was soothing all the same.

"I can confirm that Ms. Coleman and Mr. Simmons were both students here, Detective. What sort of information were you looking for exactly?" She hummed between words.

"I'm not sure exactly." I blurted out.

"I could send you a copy of their transcripts, with the proper request forms of course," she offered. "A simple letter on your department's stationery will be fine."

"That would be truly kind of you. I'll see that the proper papers are faxed to your office by Monday. Thank you again."

I called Lou at home and told him what I needed. He cursed me twice before promising to get the forms sent out that day. An hour later I passed out on the couch again.

SEVENTEEN

I arrived at police headquarters at two-thirty on Monday. The golden morning sun had been replaced by an ever-darkening sky. I sat for a moment in the parking space, enjoying my favorite Sting song, *Sister Moon*, on the radio when a severe thunderstorm alert interrupted. On a day like this I could sit at home with all the windows open and play something moody and dark against the sound of the thunder. It was a good time to purge and cleanse my soul of all the pain and frustration. God knows I needed more rain in my life.

I found Lou in the company of two stiff shirts. The first guy had to be a fed. His square, clenched jaw gave off a hard confidence. The other guy didn't come off quite as tough. He was lean and short with thinning brown hair. He had the look of a man who knew more than he should about other people's lives while at the same time being deftly afraid something might crawl out of his closet and reveal his own secrets to the world.

"Hey Gitz, I'm glad you're here." Lou jumped out of his chair like we hadn't seen each other in years. He grabbed my hand and shook it like a politician. He patted my back and leaned closer. "Help me out with these jackasses," he whispered next to my ear. He turned, speaking a little above normal volume. "This is Special Agent Fielding with the Treasury department and Mr. Bellows with the S.E.C. They'd like to ask you a few questions about the Carole Spenser case."

Lou returned to the chair behind his desk and I stood beside him, as they each nodded at me from their seats.

"We understand you and the late Ms. Spenser were involved." Fielding, the tough one, began. "We'd like to know the nature of your association with her."

I opened my mouth but Lou cut me off before I could answer.

"I told them you'd be more than happy to help them in any way." The uneasy look in his eyes convinced me to go along with him.

I faked a smile. "Sure. Anything to help."

Fielding took out a tablet from a briefcase. He used a stylus to tap a few times. "We understand you were found in bed with Ms. Spenser and later charged with her murder. Then the case was dropped at the preliminary hearing. Why?"

"Because I didn't do it," I said flatly.

He looked up at me briefly and then returned to his screen. He wrote on it with the stylus like it was paper. I rarely trust a man who relies too much on technology.

"Did Ms. Spenser ever mention any illegal dealings she may have been involved in that you recall?" He remained focused on the screen.

"I take it this has something to do with the ten-million-dollar discrepancy no one seems to be able to account for?"

Fielding looked up from his screen, attempting a poker face to hide his shock.

"How do you know about that?" Bellows' hair almost stood up on top of his head.

"Reliable source. Look, maybe if you guys filled me in—"

"—We'd prefer it if we asked the questions, Mr. Gideon." Fielding interjected. "From what we understand you're not quite out of the woods yet."

Two minutes and already I didn't like this guy. "Since you seem to know so much about me, how come you don't know about my relationship with Carole Spenser?"

"Don't play games with me, mister." He pointed the stylus at me. "I can make your life exceptionally difficult with one phone call."

I picked up the phone on Lou's desk and held the receiver up for Fielding. "You want to dial or shall I?"

"Gentlemen," Lou held up his hands, "May I remind you we're all here to work together?"

"If you're involved in this mister," Fielding added. "I could have you thrown in jail and brought up on felony charges for obstruction."

"Do it," I stepped forward and got in his face. "Then watch ten million walk right out of the country."

"All right, this has gone far enough!" Bellows finally joined the fray. "Fielding, this is getting us nowhere. What's it gonna take for you to tell us what we want to know, Mr. Gideon?"

Lou nodded at me and I put the phone back down.

"You think Carole Spenser ripped off her clients. Why?" I said.

Bellows looked at Fielding as if waiting for him to approve what he was about to tell me, but Fielding gave no agreeable sign.

"We didn't catch it right away. It took a few months for us to figure out there was something going on."

"Catch on to what?" I asked, crossing my arms.

Bellows dug into his own briefcase, flipped open a folder, and pointed to some figures on a form. "There were discrepancies in a number of profit statements from her clients. In some cases, the amount of profit they actually made was double that they reported initially. Since most of their profits from stock transactions are recorded almost immediately, it was just a matter of time before we'd catch it. But we've never seen this done on such a large scale. I mean, transactions of a couple hundred thousand dollars is a bit unusual for one trader to do on a weekly basis."

"Ms. Spenser was getting access to her clients' accounts and withdrawing more than they approved," Fielding added.

"How is that possible?" Lou queried.

"It's quite simple really, all a trader has to do is get the client's approval to access the account," Bellows continued. "They technically have full access to the funds but they're only allowed to take an approved amount. From what we gather, she got her clients' approval to enter their accounts and took what she wanted. Once she made enough for herself, she'd return the overage and, tack on a nice and in most cases, accurate profit from the amount she originally requested."

"You said it took you a few months to catch this?"

"Not everyone receives a profit and loss statement at the same time," Bellows explained. "But after a few of her clients discovered they owed more to the I.R.S. than they expected to pay, we knew there was a problem. It was only a week ago that we realized just how big the problem was."

"And she did this often enough to make ten million dollars without anybody knowing?" Lou stammered.

"She bought securitized assets in her client's name—mortgages bundled together usually—then sold them at the right price and pocketed the excess profit." Fielding tapped and scrolled down the screen on his tablet. "Banks and investment firms stopped using the old way of filing documents and started using an electronic registration system called MERS."

"What's MERS?" I asked.

"The Mortgage Electronic Registration System. After they deregulated stocks, homes could be sold as securities," Bellows explained. "But since it took time to get the docs notarized, the banks invented MERS. They just assigned a number to an instrument and used that number for all transactions. We're talking billions of dollars a day. That much money could make for a nice nest egg for a cute couple, unless one of them gets greedy."

"Your point being?" I sneered. Lou frowned at me and I tried to lower my eyebrows.

Fielding glared in my direction. "Carole Spenser gets murdered and you're found with her dead body. Do I have to do a song and dance? Maybe sharing that much money was more than you could handle?"

"Where do they grow people like you, Fielding?"

"Okay, we told you what we know." Bellows leaned forward to block my view of Fielding. "So give us something."

Bellows wasn't as bad as his buddy. Behind those wire rimmed glasses lay hidden a guy who tried hard to do his job without being a dick. People like that are rare and needed in this world.

"First of all, the woman you think is responsible wasn't Carole Spenser, her real name was Jesse Coleman. I've got a feeling that she was also one of Carole's clients. My hunch is that she was either being blackmailed into ripping off her clients or she had a partner."

Fielding raised an eyebrow. "You got any proof of either of your hunches?"

"I thought I did until she got killed last night." I stared out the window at the heavy grey clouds. "A receptionist at Prentiss had reason to believe that something shady was going on with another trader, someone who Jesse had known from their Chicago office."

"That's where we first picked up her trail." Bellows' face came alive with color as he scanned the page in the file. "Five clients, more than half a million in transaction discrepancies."

"Before she was killed, Kelly—the receptionist—told me that she had given a check to a trader who became enraged upon receiving it. She overheard him talking to someone about doing something that could have been dangerous. I think he killed her believing she had heard more than she did."

Fielding leaned forward, stylus at the ready. "This trader got a name?"

"Derek Simmons." I stared back at Fielding.

Lou turned to me. "You didn't mention this last night?"

"Yeah-well, last night I wasn't quite myself. Good thing I had somebody around to set me straight," I smiled at him. "By the way, the check to the trader was drawn on an account in the name of Jesse Coleman. Unless Derek's found a way to get it all, chances are most of the money is still there."

I watched as a smile found its way to Bellows' rosy cheeks. Even Fielding smirked a bit as he tapped away on his tablet. I reflected again on Jordan's speech about justice and revenge. I also remembered the things Lou recounted about the nature of police work and about myself. It made me feel good to prove Jordan wrong.

Lou's phone suddenly interrupted our meeting. Bellows and Fielding huddled themselves off in a corner to discuss what they had learned. Lou grunted to the affirmative every few seconds, balancing the phone between his neck and shoulder while he scribbled on a note pad. I was content to observe them all and at the same time I reflected on Jordan's catching me in Carole's apartment.

"Hot damn!" Lou slammed the phone down and snatched his jacket from behind his chair. "Gentlemen, if you will excuse me," he said to Bellows and Fielding.

"Where's the fire, Lou?" I asked.

"You're with me Gitz. We gotta move now." He struggled to get both arms in his jacket. "I just got a call from one of our cruisers near campus. We may have the car involved in last night's hit and run. I need you to ID the vehicle," he said.

He didn't have to ask me twice.

EIGHTEEN

I didn't pay much attention to the dark sky looming overhead, or the occasional flash of lighting jumping from cloud to cloud. Everything looked grey and cold, yet the air felt warm and thick with humidity. We were one block south of the Ohio State University campus, parked across the street from a yogurt shop and a dry cleaners. Normally, High Street would be jammed with students going back and forth between classes. But the populace scattered to the four corners of the globe during the summer, and only the diligent and desperate remained to suffer the season's wrath.

Lou was among the miserable during this time of year. Without an air conditioner to cool him or a fan blowing in his face, he became a total wreck. Just his luck that the air in his car wasn't working. The sweat poured from him like beer from an open keg, which only made him more irritable than usual. He was always in a huff about something. Maybe because it gave him an excuse to smoke as often as he did. I learned long ago that commenting in any fashion on the state of Lou's health was unwise and audibly hazardous.

"God, I hate this weather." He wrenched his hands against the steering wheel. He reached over me into the glove box for a takeout napkin to wipe his face. "How come you're not burning up?"

"It's all in the mind, Lou," I leaned back. "If you don't think you're hot, you're not."

"Sounds like a bunch of crap to me." He raked at his face several times, then slowed his sedan and pointed. "Is that the car?"

I squinted. The car in question was a white, two-door Mercury sedan with one of those vinyl roof coverings that had faded from poor maintenance. It had dull tires and needed a good scrubbing. The human-sized dent on the hood told me all I needed to know, even though I had only caught a glimpse of it at night, I recognized the car that killed Kelly.

"I'm pretty sure, but I'd like to get a closer look."

"Nada. You go walking up eyeing that car and the killer might decide to leave it and skip town," Lou heaved.

"Did you run the plates?" I replied, hoping he wouldn't remind me that I'd only caught a partial.

"We're already on it. But so far, nothing. Just sit tight and wait for somebody to jump in the damned thing." He eased back into the seat, his stomach almost contacting the steering wheel.

"How's the diet going?" I smiled.

"The hell with the diet," he spouted. "Between the diet and Sarah on me about cholesterol and fiber and whatever else she reads about—I'm startin' to get an ulcer."

"How is Sarah doing?"

"Bring your ass by the house more often and you'd know." He stuck his finger in my side. "She's starting to hint around about me retiring again. God, I hate when she does that. Florida brochures lying all over the place, travel packs and motor homes. God, I hate those things! You'd think she could get used to the idea that I just want to be a cop and leave it at that. Why is she always trying to change me?"

"If you're looking for marital advice Lou, I am definitely the wrong guy. I sometimes wish I could find a woman as good as Sarah. Sands was good to me, don't get me wrong. But she really didn't fit into the lifestyle of a cop's wife. Some days it was hard to leave the job and just be a good husband. Sometimes I wonder whether I liked being a cop more than I liked being married."

"Hell, who doesn't." Lou sighed. "You think you can have some kid wave a gun in your face and then go home and not have things go crazy? You think you can put some rapist down and then go home and make love to the wife? This job takes its toll on all of us, kid. Maybe that's why we turn to one another so often, maybe it's why people outside the job can't deal with how we relieve the stress. Maybe some of us get too close."

"Why do I get the feeling that we're not talking about you and Sarah or me and Sandy anymore?"

"I'm not saying anything Gitz, not really," he avoided my eyes.

"Look, I haven't even talked to Jacks in over a year. How come everybody keeps wondering whether or not we're still screwing around? That was two years ago!" I griped.

"Look, forget I said anything, okay?" He worked his way back up in his seat. "Hey, somebody's coming out of the cleaners."

I figured Lou just wanted an exit to get out of our fight about Jacks. Perhaps it was for the best anyway. I studied the woman who came out of the cleaners, skipping toward the parking lot. Something looked familiar about her, something about the way she walked, as if she tried too hard to draw attention to herself. Her hips moved rhythmically back and forth and her shoulders did their best to match the beat of her walk. Where had

I seen this stride before? It finally struck me where I'd met this woman when I noticed the neon headband she was wore.

"That's Joan Richards."

"Who the hell is Joan Richards?" Lou huffed.

I didn't pay attention to Lou as we watched Joan cross the parking lot and stop in front of the Mercury. I felt my heart jump as she slid in behind the wheel. Why was she driving the car that killed Kelly? I suddenly recalled Dr. Kamen's report. Neither Carole nor Derek worked where chloroform would be readily available. But Joan Richards did. Rather than sit there and wonder all day, I decided to just ask Joan why.

"Where the hell are you going?" Lou shouted as I got out of the car. "Are you crazy? She'll see you!"

There wasn't time to be subtle about this and I had questions for Joan that couldn't wait. I dodged past oncoming traffic into the parking lot just as Joan approached the exit. Could she have been involved in Carole's murder somehow? And if not, did she know who was? I threw up my hands as I crossed her path.

"Joan! Eddie Gideon, hold up!" I called out.

Her eyes widened at the sight of me. Her face shook as though she saw some unspeakable horror. Then the car's engine roared to life as she hit the gas. There wasn't time to dive to one side. I rolled onto the hood and slid off to the right of the car as she turned into the street. I could feel my gun cut into my chest as I fell to the street. Damn, it hurt. I couldn't think about the pain, the blood staining my shirt. I had to get to Joan. Lou jumped out of the car as I forced myself upward.

I cursed myself as I limped back to him and dropped in the car like a sack of potatoes. "Go after her!" I groaned. "Don't let her get away."

Lou caught sight of my wound as he started the car. "Jesus, you're bleeding, Gitz."

"Don't let her get away!" I winced as I pulled at my gun. The butt had cut into me further than I thought. "Let's go."

As we careened into the street, Lou called in for any other units in the area, as I took some napkins from the glovebox to put pressure on the bleeding. He started the siren and lights, and zigzagged through traffic to catch up. My chest throbbed and my knuckles ached where the skin had been torn. A bruise swelled on my forehead and the ride on Joan's car left my head anything but clear.

Suddenly, we came to a dead stop in the middle of an intersection. I held up my head and searched the street to my right as Lou did the same on the left. I had trouble focusing my sight, but I could still see no sign of Joan. The sound of Lou's fist against the dash told me he couldn't see her either. I had screwed up. She was obviously involved in this. And now she knew we were on to her. The blood stain got bigger on my shirt as I leaned into the door and cursed myself again. And the rain began to fall.

NINETEEN

"It's protocol. You were hit by a car for god sakes! We've got a dozen other uniforms looking for her."

Lou insisted I get the once-over for my injuries, and despite his carelessness with his own health, there was no point in arguing with him. Thankfully the hospital deemed I was fine. No concussion, a few minor scrapes and a mere three stitches in my chest. Normally the fuss over some superficial injuries would irritate me, but today I could've kissed Lou's forehead! We got the skinny on Joan Richards from a chatty ER resident. Turned out Joan was an RN at St. Paul's until a few days ago when she abruptly quit without an explanation or two weeks' notice. As we hurried out of the hospital, two thoughts crossed my mind about the significance of Joan's sudden departure.

Both of them led back to Prentiss Securities, where the new receptionist, Heather Hancock, greeted Lou and me. Heather lacked her predecessor's charm, and she seemed most efficient in taking over and removing all remnants of Kelly. Her desk overflowed with volumes of Marie Clare, Elle, and Vogue, and an enormous, designer knock-off handbag. It was near sacrilege to see this over-baked tart in Kelly's chair.

"Can I help you?" she asked without any enthusiasm.

"Lieutenant Lou Brandon." Lou flashed his badge. "We're here to see Derek Simmons."

"I'm afraid that's impossible," she said, pushing herself back into her chair as she took a brief assessment of her nails. "Derek Simmons doesn't work here anymore."

"What? Since when?" I leaned forward making my presence known.

She moved her head about like a dashboard bobble head bouncing down the road. "Since today, Derek resigned this afternoon. A real shame if you ask me, he's so cute and everything. A guy like that can get almost anything he wants, y'know?" She seemed to drift away in her thoughts, winding her blonde hair around her finger. "It's a shame."

"This ain't looking good at all," Lou huffed.

"Joan must have gotten to him before we did." I turned back to Heather. "What time did Derek actually leave the building?" I asked.

"It had to be around 4:30. My girlfriend Judy usually calls me then, and I remember seeing him leave. I was telling Judy how he tries to pretend he doesn't notice me but—"

"—It's already been thirty-five minutes." Lou cut her off. He tapped his cell and started barking orders. "Yeah—I need an APB out on Joan Richards and Derek Simmons. I want officers at the airport and bus stations. Richards is a white female, late 30s, shoulder-length red hair. Last seen driving the Mercury from yesterday's hit-and-run. You've got Derek's sheet. Unknown if they're together, but likely. Consider them both armed and dangerous."

I nodded. "Might not be a bad idea to let the Feds know what's going on. We might need their help." I pulled out my cell and tapped Bellows' number.

"I dunno Gitz, this is really startin' to stink." Lou shook his head.

***

For the past five hours, we staked out Joan's place on the chance she might return. Lou and I, along with two other officers, roosted in a surveillance van hoping she'd show. Undercover cops staked out St. Paul's Hospital in the event that she went back there. The police and Feds had similar stakeouts at Derek's apartment, Prentiss Securities, as well as the airport, car rental agencies, bus stations, and train station. The Feds even had a helo searching from the sky. It was nearly ten-thirty and so far we had zip.

No one took any bets on either of them showing up, but I had a feeling she would. She didn't seem to be dull-witted, but she wasn't a professional criminal. Perhaps she didn't see herself as a criminal at all and had no reason not to return home. Whatever the reason, I was hoping she would come back.

I still tried to piece together Joan's role in all of this. She claimed not to have known Carole very well, but it seemed she'd been lying. Maybe she had told me the truth in the sense that she didn't know Carole. But did she know Jesse? In either case, I was sure she and Derek had acted together. As a nurse, she was the most likely suspect to have access to chloroform—and it was a smart choice because most medical examiners test for more commonly used drugs like GHB, rather than something old school like chloroform. Could she have been the person Kelly overheard Derek arguing with? But how could she get access to Jesse's account?

With no activity outside the van, Lou and I traded bad jokes and lousy coffee with Sampson and Marren, the same officers who arrested me a few days ago. At first they acted a bit skittish of me, especially Sampson. He didn't know what to make of me cozying up to his boss. He gave me a generic apology about his attitude the morning they found me in Carole's bed. I gave him my lack-luster acceptance, and after a while they loosened up. Some interesting stories came out of these two officers. But none more interesting than what they told us about the morning they arrested me.

"So, Jim and I are about to stop for the day when the call comes in. We were in the area, so we took the call," Sampson explained. He still didn't like me much and wasn't too pleased that Lou allowed me to tag along on the stakeout.

Marren gave me a sheepish look. "No offense Gideon, but when we busted in and found you in bed with the body, we thought you were some kind of pervert, one of those weirdos that gets off on dead bodies."

I stifled a laugh. "So just out of the blue, you guys get a tip that someone's been murdered, bust in, find me in bed with a dead woman, and nobody wonders why?"

"Like I said, we were freaked out a little," Marren shuddered. "You don't see that kind of thing every day."

"Amen to that," Lou sipped his coffee. "I'd lose my cookies if I had to see you naked," he grinned.

"You'd be jealous, you old fart." I pointed my finger at him. "So who called in the complaint?"

"911 Dispatch said a woman heard noises." Sampson leaned up from the back seat.

"A woman reported the noises?"

Marren looked at me. "Is that important?"

"Did anyone run out to meet you guys when you showed up?"

Sampson shook his head. "Everything was quiet when we arrived. We found the door to the victim's apartment open. We called out a few times and went in."

"But you guys didn't run into anybody nosing about the place when you got there?"

He shook his head again. "Nope. Come to think of it, that is odd. Usually worried neighbors are waiting for us."

"Yeah, if there's one neighbor concerned enough to call, other neighbors are at least peeking out their windows, right?"

"Exactly." I recalled Joan saying she had worked a double the night of the murder. If a gunshot didn't wake the entire complex, then chances were Derek had arranged to have her make the call. I had a theory now as to what might have happened that night, but I'd need Joan to fill in a few blanks.

"Can you get dispatch to tell us where the 911 call came from, Lou?" I asked.

"Shouldn't take too long, sure." He swiped his phone and put in the request.

A few other thoughts crossed my mind as we huddled together in the darkness. But they had nothing to do with Derek or Carole. I'd almost forgotten what it was like to be on a stakeout—lousy food and long hours. Just the sound of your partner's voice to keep you awake. Memories of arguing with Jacks snuck up on me and made me wonder, which in itself was a dangerous thing. The last time Jacks and I let our curiosity get the better of us, it cost us both our marriages.

Elayne Jackson and I became partners shortly after the incident with Petey and that whole scandal. Jacks made good company and she did something Sands had lost her patience for: she listened to me. Jacks would let me go on for hours about whatever was on my mind, whatever I could think to say to her. The only time she ever told me to shut up was the night she first kissed me. I guess I should have let it go at that, but being that close to someone, someone like Jacks, you just can't walk away from that.

Lou could've been right about the stress of the job making us turn to one another when our life partners couldn't make sense of what we went through. Maybe we got closer than we should have. Maybe it was the faulty squad car heater in the height of winter that made us fantasize about being anywhere else. Maybe we told one too many jokes, kissed once too often that night. But then neither of us believed that what happened one night would destroy so many lives. Neither of us knew we would cause so much pain.

"I'll be damned." Lou suddenly sat upright.

I leaned over to see what had him so alive all of a sudden. I had to hand it to the old man, even though it was dark out and the car came up quietly with its lights down, Lou had spotted Joan trying to make her way unnoticed, back to her apartment.

"We've got movement," Marren announced.

I opened the van door as Joan turned into her complex. "Rule number four guys, ain't no such thing as a sure thing."

Lou followed my move while Marren and Sampson informed dispatch and the other teams.

"Robin's approaching the nest."

"Requesting back up at Robin's nest."

I knew I should've let Lou and the guys just bring her down, but I had this need to tell her how much I enjoyed the ride we shared that afternoon. Besides, she owed me for the stitches. I crept down and made my way across the street to a thick hedge. Lou slid up beside me and then signaled Sampson to head around the back. The rest was simple. We waited for Joan to go inside and then Lou, Marren, and I ran up and flanked her door. Inside we could hear Joan going through the place like a professional wrestler in a grudge match.

I side-stepped to keep one eye on the door and one on the front window, trampling the geraniums and azaleas in front of the unit. Joan's shadow moved frantically across the bay window, but never peered out. The sound of breaking glass masked the scratchy sound of Lou's Two-Way that protruded from his hip. Sampson reported he was in position.

"Then pipe down and stay hid." Lou growled softly. All of a sudden a cheesy kind of grin oozed its way across his face. He was looking at me in a strange way now, almost giddy.

"What?" I asked.

"Feels good, don't it?" He checked his gun. "Back in the saddle?"

"For Pete's Sake Lou, get a grip," I whispered.

"Tell me you don't get a rush from being back in the game again?"

"I can't believe this. There is a crazy woman inside here who tried to kill me, and you want to know if I'm getting my rocks off from being bent over her door?" I wanted to scream.

"Feels good, don't it?"

"You are a perverted old man with a sick sense of humor." I pointed sharply. "You need help."

"Don't you miss it?" His madness knew no end. "The thrill of the chase? The moment just before you take a suspect down when the adrenaline nearly sets you on fire? You gotta love it."

"Louis Brandon, go to hell."

Lou started to respond, but then loud banging noises, like trash cans tumbling, erupted from the back. Lou pressed himself against the wall. He muttered a few other choice expletives as Marren and I hit the ground and moved beneath the bay window. He squeezed his shoulders between a dark crevice that separated the apartments.

Suddenly the glow from the lights inside was snuffed out. Joan must have heard the noise out back. Her frantic steps became slow and almost unnoticeable. Even though I couldn't see her, I knew she was checking every window, looking for us moving about in the darkness.

"Shit." Lou cursed from across her door.

Next we heard the sound of the door being gingerly pulled open. It looked like Joan planned to bolt. Lou crouched half-in, half-out of the shadows. I rolled up to my knees, ready to spring like a cat. Joan crept out into the night, slowly at first, surveying the area as best she could. She had only herself to blame that she didn't notice me. She carried two large boxes, both of them overstuffed with things I could barely make out in the darkness. The bulk of it inhibited her field of view and allowed me to walk right up to her. This time though, I wasn't about to let her run me down.

"Stop right there, Joan." I held my gun at arm's length.

She dropped her load at once. "Oh my God! Help! Please don't kill me!" she screamed.

"Police!" Lou burst from the shadows. "Joan Richards, you're under arrest for the murder of Kelly Greer." He held both his badge and his gun in plain sight to emphasize the futility of resistance.

Joan's face lit up with the lights of a squad car as it barreled into the courtyard. Sampson came huffing from around the back. He knew from the look on Lou's face that Lou would have a word or two with him later. With all the badges around, I decided my part of the gunplay was over and put away my Baretta.

"You have the right to remain silent..." Lou began.

"But I didn't do anything." Tears started to roll down her face. "God as my witness, I didn't do anything!"

"So you were just saying hello when you tried to run me down?" I said bitterly. "That your way of greeting people?"

"I—I thought you were going to hurt me." She wept openly as Lou finished reading her rights. Marren guided her toward the wall to frisk her for any concealed weapons.

"I thought you were going to kill me like you killed Carole!" she howled.

"Is that why you ran down a helpless girl, Joan?" I wanted to break her. "Did you think she was trying to kill you too, or was it something else?"

"God please, I didn't do anything!" Tears streaked down her face.

I wedged my way between Joan and Marren. "You're a liar, Joan. You're guilty, and you're going to prison for murder. Do you have any idea what they'll do to you in prison? No more young boys to tell you how beautiful you are, Joan." I grabbed her by the arms. "All those years you've tried to cheat the clock ain't gonna mean a damn thing in the joint! By the time you get out, you won't remember what it's like to have a man hold you."

"No! No, you don't understand! It's not my fault!"

"Same damned car, Joan!" I shouted back. "Your car was the same damned car that killed Kelly, the same car that tried to run me down earlier today. The same car I will identify when they haul you into court for murder."

"Gitz, that's enough!" Lou called out.

Joan's tears had made a mess of her face. Dark lines ran from her eyes and stained her cheeks. Her lipstick looked as though it had been applied with a scouring pad. The woman who once exuded self-confidence was now a humbled, shallow figure of fear. I had done my damnedest to break her and make her feel helpless. This sort of thing usually went against the grain for me, but I knew she was our only link to Derek.

"I feel sorry for you." I shook my head. "Goodbye, Joan."

I turned to Lou as Marren escorted Joan to the squad car. He knew what I was up to though, from the frown on his face. I'm not sure he genuinely believed my little gambit would work. But then again, I'd already bet on Joan once.

"Wait! You can't do this!" Joan called to me. "All I did was take some stuff from the hospital. I only gave him some drugs, that's all. It wasn't me!"

Lou eyes widened at Joan's words. He waved for Marren to bring Joan back to us. Lou figured it was his turn now to play the heavy.

"Why should we believe it wasn't you?" Lou glared at her.

"All right, I got scared when I saw you." She turned to me. "But I didn't kill the other person, this Kelly? I swear to you I was at the hospital until midnight."

I had her scared now. "Who did you lend your car to, Joan?"

She turned to Lou now. "You've got to understand, he thought someone was trying to kill him. He got scared. He didn't know. There were things going on you don't understand."

I stared at her, unwilling to let go. "It was Derek. He had your car last night."

"He told me you were dangerous. He said you'd killed Carole. He said we had to get out of town."

"Where is he?" Lou asked.

"Please, he'll kill me if I turn on him," she pleaded with us. "You don't know how good he's been to me."

I took her by the arm again. "Derek has already killed two women, do you really think he gives a shit about you? He used you from the start.

If you think he's planning to spend his life with you, forget it. You're as good as dead yourself. He'll kill you the first chance he gets."

Lou sighed. "Time's running out, Ms. Richards."

"Joan, please."

Joan's eyes darted back and forth between Lou and me. She wiped her tears, spreading the dark mascara across her cheeks. Lou handed her his handkerchief and she gently wiped her nose. She sighed as she tried to compose herself.

"What do I have to do?"

TWENTY

The Brewery District lay south of downtown. The stretch of brownstones and rowhouses had become the mecca for the professional Millennial contingent. The place looked like a New England postcard. Red brick streets lined with a predictable mix of Lexus, BMW, and upper-end EV and hybrid cars parked beneath old fashioned lanterns that hung like tear drops from black iron posts. The rent here ran triple what people just a few blocks away managed to afford. Hard to believe that a few years ago this whole area had been nothing more than a bunch of run down and abandoned warehouses. Now it was the second highest rent district in the city and the sanctuary of the Nouveau Riche. How appropriate that Derek would be hiding here.

Joan might have been gullible where Derek was concerned, but she wasn't stupid. Not only had she told us where to find Derek, she led the way. Joan also cleared up a couple of loose ends for me. I'd guessed correctly that she provided Derek with the chloroform to knock me out the night he killed Carole. But Joan had been just a minor player, a pathetic puppet in all of this. That bastard Derek had her wound up like a music box.

Sgt. Hamp Baker marched up to Lou and me. Baker headed the police SWAT Unit. Tall and rigid, with sharp, even shoulders, Baker looked like the kind of man who took buying toilet paper seriously. He didn't have so much as a speck of lint on his black uniform and you could bet he demanded the same from his subordinates.

"My team is in position, Lieutenant." Baker sounded as though he had spoken through a megaphone once too often. "We can do this any way you like. I've got a sniper—"

"—A sniper? I thought you weren't going to kill him!" Fear shot through Joan's voice.

She stood close to me with the look of a frightened child. She was still under the impression that we, and not Derek, were the villains here. Stress brought worried lines across her face and made her hands tremble the way people ten years her senior did. I felt half bad for her.

"No one is trying to kill him, ma'am," Lou tried to reassure her. "The sergeant was just saying how well his men are organized."

"How are we going to get him out, Lou?"

It didn't seem like a terrible question to ask, but Lou pulled me away from the group and kept his voice low. "Gitz, this is where you get off the bus. Go home."

"What the hell are you talking about?"

"What I'm talking about is you not being around when we go in after this guy. I know you've got a stake in this, but I should've yanked you out a long time ago. Bottom line is you believe this guy killed your girlfriend. And I'm not gonna give you a chance to do something stupid."

"Lou, for God's sake."

"I mean it Gitz. You get in my car and go home or I swear—"

"—Lieutenant. He's coming out," Baker alerted Lou and silently signaled his team to move on his command.

My heart jumped at the sight of Derek heading for his car. It was like watching a precision surgery as the team moved in and out of the shadows without Derek noticing. Lou gave me an angry look, but what could he do? A part of me wanted to run out and go a few more rounds with the bastard, but common sense made me stay put. Whatever happened next, I'd be there for it.

Lou took the megaphone Baker held out to him and called to Derek. "Derek Simmons, stop where you are. This is the police. We have you surrounded. Put your hands above your head. Do not move or try to run away. Stay absolutely still and no one will get hurt."

It all should have gone down easy, but then suddenly two unmarked cars roared down the street toward Derek, sliding against the brick streets. They were neither Lou's men nor Baker's. It had to be the Feds.

"What the fuck is this?" Lou snarled.

Special Agent Fielding came off like Wyatt Earp as he jumped from his car, drawing down on Derek. "F.B.I. Put your hands up!"

"Fielding, you fuck-up!" Lou yelled.

Shit. This had all gone wrong. Fielding, who turned to Lou, didn't have the presence of mind to keep his gun poised on Derek who whipped out a piece and started shooting at anything that moved. He crouched behind his open car door to keep from getting hit. Suddenly the street came alive with gunfire. Dammit, this wasn't supposed to happen.

"Derek! Nooo!" Joan screamed.

Baker's men fumbled between the antics of Fielding and his posse. Lou was furious and I couldn't blame him. Derek had been a hair's breadth away from being arrested. In the confusion, no one thought to keep Joan out of the way. I should've grabbed her before she bolted toward Derek. Someone had to stop her. I just hoped I could get to her before either of us would catch a bullet.

"Hold your fire!" Lou shouted. "Hold your fire!"

My heart beat against my chest like a baseball bat on a brick wall. Joan had a short stride but her steps were quick. Guns were firing all around. All I had to do was reach out and pull her down to the ground until the shooting stopped. Just three steps and it would all be over.

"Derek wait!" she yelled to him.

Derek turned, his gun still shaking in his hand. At that moment, I wasn't sure if he was pointing it at me or at Joan. I had to move fast or one of us would find out the hard way. I yanked out my gun and prayed I was a better shot than Derek.

"Joan, get down!" I yelled.

Recognition suddenly exploded in Derek's eyes. With Joan in the way I didn't have a clear shot, and now I was sure he had me lined up in his sights. I tried to brace, anticipating the shot when Derek suddenly twisted upright. His gun fired, one shot striking the ground. Then he twisted again, as if someone had stabbed him in the back. I stopped just behind Joan and pushed her down. I had a clear shot at him, but I hesitated for a moment, something about the way he stood there now, as though he had suddenly become incoherent.

"Derek?" Joan's voice trembled.

I turned behind me and saw Baker waving off one of his officers. I turned again and saw a man rise from the top of one of the buildings. The sniper.

Derek slumped to the ground. FBI agents and police moved in around us as I lifted Joan into a waiting officer's arms. I moved to Derek's side, kneeling down as he struggled for air and some sense of comfort. The sniper's aim was perfect, two clean hits to the back. Derek lay dying.

"Try not to move," I said despite myself. I didn't owe this guy a bit of sympathy, not after what he'd done to me, and worse, to Carole. I wanted all the decency to run out of me so I could kick the hell out of him with a clear conscience.

"Damned shame, ain't it?" he said between gasps.

"What do you mean?"

His chest heaved as he struggled to catch his breath. Once or twice his eyes rolled back as though he were about to lose consciousness. Derek put his hand against one of his wounds. Blood was saturating his shirt and stomach.

He turned his head to the left in my direction. "Carole, she made suckers out of both of us."

The next moment he was gone. The man who killed Carole and Kelly had finally paid for his crimes. As ambulance sirens approached, I knew there no longer was a need for any heroic attempts to resuscitate. They would simply document the official time and declare that Derek Simmons was dead.

Lou held his own in a shouting match with Special Agent Fielding. Somebody would have to take the blame for this mess, and for a change it wasn't me. An officer ushered Joan away to answer for her part in all of this. A part of me wished I could do something for her. I gave her a half shrug as she caught sight of me just before they put her in the squad car. She had lost everything. Her love, and her freedom. It's always love or money. In this case, both. The consequences of everything that had just happened paled compared to what she lost.

I nodded with respect as Baker approached me.

"Sometimes no matter what you do," he said. "It's a no-win situation. You simply do the job. Terminate the threat and move on."

His words left me cold. I had the feeling he regarded people as cockroaches infesting his locker. He didn't have any feeling about the people he went after. He saw them as merely troublesome things that didn't belong in his world. That scared me. But I could agree with the moving on part. Carole's killer had been caught. I would be cleared of the murder, and though it was a hollow victory, it was a sign that I could go on with my life again.

TWENTY-ONE

I awoke feeling worse than when I went to bed. I stayed up most of the night after Derek's death, giving my statement to an officer who seemed as happy to see me as I was to smell his stale breath. All of that, and my final summation with Lou and briefing the FBI, totaled just over three and a half hours.

Derek was carrying fifty thousand dollars in cash when they caught him. The police found plane tickets, passbooks for some foreign bank accounts, and some other documents the FBI would have to sort through to track down the missing ten million. Bellows mentioned something about a record of transfers to various accounts and something about bearer bonds that might lead them to the money. I was more than a little disappointed they didn't find the gun he used to kill Jesse. Fielding was surprised Derek wasn't carrying the whole load on him. Foolish thinking on his part, I thought. Derek was desperate but he wasn't stupid. I don't think anyone in their right mind would walk around with that much cash in their back pocket. Still, one had to wonder, where was the money?

I dragged myself down to Deacon's, drifting somewhere between sleep and my seventh cup of coffee. I sat down at the piano on the bandstand.

I hoped that with this whole mess over, things would somehow return to normal. I was ready for everything to slip back into standard mode. I began playing a piece that I'd been mulling over for the last few weeks. A set of descending chords I couldn't quite find a resolution for and wasn't making much headway.

"Little early for that, don't you think?" John waltzed through the door. He had a blueberry muffin in one hand and a bag with more in the other. He wore black jeans with a loose-fitting grey shirt, a bone-colored tie and matching suspenders. Even when he dressed casually, he always looked first class.

"Where you been?" he asked.

"Here and there, trying to shut this murder thing down in my head." I continued to struggle with the chords.

"They caught the guy?" he raised an eyebrow.

"Derek Simmons, killed last night. He tried to shoot it out and got nailed," I said.

"Damned shame. I would have liked to have known why he did what he did," he leaned over the piano.

"Ten million dollars. What's to know?" I shrugged.

He gave me a slack-jawed look. "You seem awfully edgy today. And your playing lacks depth and sincerity in ways one can sense from the arc of your hands," His eyes widened with each word.

"How 'bout you kiss my ass with depth and sincerity?" I replied. "You'd be edgy too if you spent half the night giving statements to law enforcement. Where's all this coming from?"

"Perfection. Which reminds me." He smiled and moved to the bar. He reached around and grabbed a large package, something thick and bulky. He laid the package down in front of me.

"Came for you the other day, thought it might be a piece of the puzzle or something."

Marge Barker had responded quickly to the form Lou faxed her albeit the package arrived a little late. Hopefully it would fill in the gaps about Derek and Jesse. God, I still couldn't get used to calling Carole that. I'd almost forgotten I'd asked Marge to send me what she could find.

"Who do you know in Illinois?"

"A friend." I pulled at one corner until the paper ripped a nice hole for me to dig through. "Did I get any other calls?"

"Skip wanted to know if you were done with that box of letters you took from the crime scene. He said the boys from evidence would be interested in getting a look at it."

"Jesus, I didn't know he knew I had them."

I pulled out a note from Marge. Her handwriting was clear and distinctive, neat to a fault. Slow and meticulous about every letter she laid on the page. She had addressed the note to both Lou and me.

Mr. Brandon and Mr. Gideon,

Please find the enclosed first-year record book with pictures of those students entering our school as freshmen in 2007. I have ear-marked the pages with photos of the three students you inquired about. Jesse Coleman, though she did attend for a few years, was not a graduate of our school as it turns out.

If I may be of further assistance, please do not hesitate to call upon me.

Sincerely,

Marge Barker

Clerk of Alumni Records

I shoved the package under my arm and headed for the back stairwell.

"I'll finish this in my room," I said to John.

"Yeah, hog it all for yourself, why don't you?" he half-frowned.

I was too tired to flip him the bird and more interested in looking over the pictures in the book. John would have scooted me off soon enough. He had the lunch crowd to prepare for and today was the day he went over the schedule. That always made him a real bear. Besides, I stole his last muffin.

I laid the package on top of the shoebox I borrowed from the crime scene. I still hadn't taken the time to go through Carole's letters. Perhaps I'd been avoiding that issue on purpose to keep from remembering what Carole and I shared. Memories often had the appeal of scars to me. And I wasn't one of those men who wore their scars like merit badges.

I bit into the muffin and pondered what Derek said to me before he died. Normally a thing like that wouldn't get to me, but something about his face as he laid dying bothered me. Maybe he did it just to get one last rise out of me. I never did pay him back for the shot in the mouth he gave me. The quivering in my stomach returned as I swallowed. That old queasiness I experienced a few days ago came back. A summer cold was the last thing I needed.

All of a sudden I felt fuzzy and out of focus, with an odd feeling as if I'd forgotten something important. I put on a pot of coffee and took the package and the shoebox to my desk. I began slowly going through the letters, scanning over every word. I noted sender's addresses and compared handwriting. I realized as I sorted the pictures that I no longer had the same photo I took with me when I met Cappie. He had given me the picture he had of the two of them by mistake. I picked it up along with several others in the box, wondering why I couldn't shake the unsettling feeling in my gut. I felt like a rock was about to drop on my head at any moment.

I shuffled through the pictures, the faces moving like flash cards before my eyes. Jesse Coleman and her grandfather embraced as a grandparent and grandchild should be.

Then I flipped them over, sifting through each picture like before, reading Carole's writing on each. That's when something went crazy in my head. All of the pictures read "Cappie & Me" all save the one picture Cappie gave me.

It read "Jesse and Cappie".

I don't know why that seemed odd to me but it did.

I suddenly got the feeling that I had overlooked something.

I turned the pictures back over and studied their faces now. Some of the images were old and I had to dig up my old magnifying glass to get a better look. I took the pictures and the magnifier over to the coffee table and spread the pictures out across the surface. At first I wondered whether I could still be suffering some effects from the chloroform or sleep deprivation, but Derek's voice kept repeating in my head and it was driving me crazy. Five times I covered each picture from top to bottom and still couldn't figure out what I was looking for. Then as I laid the magnifying glass down on the last picture, I found something.

In the photo Cappie gave me, Jesse wore a hat covering most of her head. Through the glass you could see a part of her hair and it was just as I remembered it, but nothing like Cappie had described. That didn't make sense. I also noticed from the date stamp on the back that the picture was several weeks old, but Cappie had said it was from two years ago. What the hell had I stumbled onto?

Suddenly my phone buzzed.

"What's up, Lou?"

"In all the excitement last night, I forgot about the 911 call Sampson and Marren responded to, Gitz. This is strange," he said.

"What do you mean, strange?"

I could hear him flick his cigarette lighter. "According to dispatch, the 911 call didn't come from our friend Joan Richards."

I sat down for what came next. "So who made the call?"

"The call came from a cell phone registered in the name of Carole Spenser. The son-of-a-bitch who framed you called after they'd knocked you out. We thought it might have been the Richards woman, but her story about being at work the night of the murder checked out," Lou exhaled. "Just when I think we're done with this, more shit comes to the surface."

"Thanks, Lou. I've gotta go. I'll call you later."

Suddenly Marge's note struck an odd chord within me. She wrote that Jesse Coleman never graduated from college, and yet I remembered Cappie leaving me a message saying that she had. I scrolled my phone and tapped my voicemail. I listened to every message I'd received in the last few days, taking care to skip past Kelly's message to me. When I reached the one Cappie left me, I listened with nervous interest.

"I've been giving the matter of why Jesse changed her name some thought, and I think you're right that she may have been trying to keep someone from finding her," he said. "I remembered a few things about a young man she dated in college. Jesse graduated from the University of Illinois back in '11. Call me soon." His voice made me tremble.

I didn't like where this was leading me. I scurried to gather the box of letters to study them more carefully now, taking the time to read the sender's names on the envelopes. I wasn't quite sure of what I had found, but I hoped to God that what I suspected was way off base. By the time I passed over half a dozen letters, my hopes had been dashed.

I learned a long time ago that criminals usually leave some clue behind about who they are, no matter how perfect the crime. And it's always something simple, something that they've taken for granted. I had come across just that kind of mistake. Cappie had led me to believe that he had no idea who Carole Spenser was, yet here in my hand I held a letter he had written to his darling granddaughter, Caroline and in it a picture of the two of them, both their names written across the back.

I remembered Marge's note saying she marked the pages of the three students I asked about. Three students.

Damn, I'd almost forgotten that I originally asked her about Carole before I asked about Jesse. I grabbed the freshman record book Marge sent me. Maybe I was wrong, God I hoped I was wrong. I flipped through the pages until I came across Jesse Coleman's picture. I went back in my mind to the body I saw in the morgue, the one in bed beside me that morning. They all had the same face, the same name. We'd identified the body as Jesse Coleman. She attended the University of Illinois with Derek. So where was the catch?

"She made suckers out of both of us." Derek's voice echoed in my mind.

I began turning pages again, slowly working my way through the M's, the P's, and the R's. My hands began trembling as I passed Sarin, Scalon, and other names and faces I never knew. But I saw one face among them I knew well, the face of the woman who captured my heart and used me like a tinker toy in her game of seduction and deception. My hands shook at the sight of her. It was Carole Spenser.

***

It took me three hours and a good bottle of whiskey to finally figure it all out. When I put the whole thing together I almost wanted to laugh. It was like something out of a movie. Jesse Coleman was for all practical purposes, Carole's double. A perfect match aside from some minor differences in hair color and eyes, they could have passed for identical twins. The resemblance was so striking that I didn't realize it when they switched and laid Jesse down next to me. No one would have questioned who she was. No one did question it. We all assumed that the body was Carole all along.

Damn, how could I have been so blind? They must have planned this for months. Carole knew she couldn't keep her scam at Prentiss going on without someone getting wise to her, perhaps it was too late for her to try to cover her tracks any other way. Somehow she and Derek got Jesse involved and killed her. Carole must have been the one who drugged me, sometime after I had fallen asleep and then brought in Jesse's body. Jesse must have been killed after they knocked me out.

It all made sense now. Carole and I would share an intimate evening at her apartment. After we had satiated our passions, Carole slipped out of bed and put her plan into motion. Derek and Jesse could have been there the whole time, or maybe Carole let them in after I was knocked out, thanks to Joan Richards. Skip had told me that Jesse had been really high, the level of cocaine in her blood might have even killed her eventually. But it also made killing her all the easier for Carole and Derek. With me out of the way and no neighbors close by to hear them, they killed Jesse and left me to hold the bag. Sampson and Marren claimed the dispatch said a woman called in the complaint. It must have been Carole herself who made the call to the police to frame me for her murder.

But somewhere along the line, Carole decided to double-cross Derek. He didn't even suspect. She must have realized that I wouldn't rest until I found out who had framed me and killed her. Perhaps she banked on it. Carole knew that I'd take it upon myself to find Cappie and bring him the news of her death. The two of them pointed me right to Derek and I followed the trail like a bloodhound. She almost got away with it. She would have if not for the pictures, the letters, and meticulous Marge Barker.

Kelly had stumbled onto part of their setup, not realizing what she found would make them kill her before she could blow their whole scheme. They killed poor Kelly for trying to help me and left her blood on my hands.

The generic definition of murder is a crime of unlawfully killing a person or persons with premeditated malice, punishable by life in prison or death. The body count was already up to three. Two innocent women, who by no fault of their own, were dead. Derek had Joan wrapped up so tight she didn't know crap from cream cheese, and thankfully her life was spared.

I was convinced of three things. One, Carole was still alive. Two, she still had what was left of the ten million. And three, she used me to help her get away with it.

I couldn't live with that.

TWENTY-TWO

I paused in front of Jordan's door, taking a final moment to be sure this was what I wanted to do, what I had to do. My tongue felt coated and the strain on my brain left me shaky and unsteady for what lay ahead. Things were starting to become clearer now. For two hours I tried to figure out what to do next, but each time I came to the same conclusion. To get Carole, I'd need help.

Jordan lived in an area of town known as Clintonville, a burb with a time-lost charm amidst the snug fitted duplexes and two-story homes. The streets were always unusually quiet. People moved slowly, like a child on a porch with an all-day sucker, watching the bumblebees skirt across the lawn.

Jordan lived in a huge duplex with a screened wooden porch divided at the center by a screened lattice, to give each neighbor a sense of privacy. The house was covered with aluminum siding, a chalky ivory color with a flat finish. Peach toned shutters brought some life to the color scheme. Plants with long green vines hung against the screen, thick and fragrant like a mini greenhouse. I grabbed a book from the passenger seat and tucked it under my arm, then walked up the steps to the righthand door. I ran my fingers against a heavy-duty plastic mailbox with the name McCrae embossed on tiny silver plates. The lights were on inside. I knocked twice and Jordan appeared.

She greeted me with a mixture of astonishment and annoyance. She twisted her mouth to one side as she stared at me curiously. She wore a sweat top, jeans, and a baseball cap. I hadn't seen her wear glasses previously, but she wore them now.

"This is a surprise," she pushed open the screen door. "A little late for a social call isn't it, Mr. Gideon?"

I was suddenly hesitant to get into it with Jordan. I even questioned why I had chosen to come to her in the first place. We hadn't known one another for very long and I couldn't even call her a friend by the most extreme stretch of the truth. With all the trouble I'd caused her in the last few days, she was justified in hating me. And yet, Jordan was the person I chose to turn to now. Maybe she was the only person I could turn to.

"That coffee I smell?" I asked.

She stared at me for what seemed like an eternity. "I just made a fresh pot. Want some?"

***

As she moved off into the kitchen, I took a moment to think of what to say to her. I still hadn't put it all together when she returned with mug in hand and a lift in one eyebrow.

"Smells great."

"You didn't come all this way just to comment on my coffee."

I avoided the question. I looked around at the spacious living room. A coffee table smothered in legal documents and a laptop, an antique loveseat under the window that overlooked the porch. To my left was a sofa, facing an enormous flat screen TV on a tasteful home entertainment console. I set the book down on the loveseat and stepped to my right to take a closer look at the framed family photos displayed on a wide mantle above a fireplace. It appeared she was the sole daughter in a large family.

"The McCrae Clan." She came over to give me a proper introduction. "The distinguished looking guy is my father James. These are my brothers Jimmy, Sam, Neal, Patrick, and my twin brother, Joey."

She moved to an older photograph at the end. "My mother, Patricia McCrae. She died when I was eight. I was the only one who didn't cry at her funeral." The tone in her voice shifted. "You can't imagine how hard she worked to keep us fed, clothed, and clean. I guess I was glad to see that she could rest at last."

"She sounds like an incredible woman," I offered softly.

Jordan smiled briefly, then that look of curiosity dropped over her once again. "Look, don't get me wrong, but was there a particular reason—I mean, why are you here?"

I sat down on the loveseat and drew a deep breath as I searched my mind for words to make sense of this. I sipped my coffee for a moment, then placed the cup on the floor beside me. I decided to just keep it simple.

"Carole Spenser is still alive."

Jordan's eyes widened as she sat on the sofa. She drove her hand through her red locks as she leaned forward, narrowing her gaze on me. "Carole Spenser and Jesse Coleman were the same person. You showed that in court. How could she still be alive?"

"It was just as much a shock to me, Jordan." I tried to avoid her angry stare.

She leaned back against the sofa. "Hold on here, I got a call the other day that Derek Simmons was the one behind this whole murder. He killed Jesse Coleman, framed you and tried to embezzle millions of dollars from Prentiss Securities. Are you saying that none of this is true?"

I drew my hand across my face, grappling for a way to explain what I was still trying to understand. I reached out and handed her the yearbook.

She gave me a puzzled look. "What's this?"

"Proof. Look up Jesse Coleman," I said.

She flipped through the pages until her finger came to rest on Jesse's picture. "Okay, so?"

"Now look up Carole Spenser."

She stared at me for a moment, blinking as though what I'd asked her to do didn't make sense. She pulled back a stack of pages and ran through a list of names, calling them out as she searched. When she found Carole's picture she looked up at me, her disbelief more intense.

"Oh my God," she whispered.

"It was all a con from the very beginning," I began again. "Everything we believed about Jesse Coleman was true to a point. She was the woman the police found dead, and I believe Derek was the guy who killed her. But what none of us knew was that there really was a Carole Spenser and she is still alive."

Jordan held up her hand before I could continue. She ran into the kitchen and then returned carrying a couple of beers. I smiled and turned down the opportunity to join her. Once over the can was enough for me. Jordan plopped back onto the sofa and took two big gulps out of the first bottle, then a shot from the other. I wondered if this was what I looked like so many hours ago.

"Lay this out for me," she managed between burps.

"Okay." I sighed. "At first I thought Derek may have been extorting Jesse. Maybe he found out she was embezzling and threatened her if she didn't cut him in. Carole's grandfather was the one who told me that Carole was really Jesse. That's how I got Melvin to pull that stunt in court. At the time, I was the only one who knew the true identity of the woman who had been murdered."

"When did you see her grandfather?"

"The day you were hunting me down with that subpoena, I took a flight to Chicago and drove down to the retirement community where he lives. I managed to get back in time to run into you at Deacon's."

"Slick little bastard," she grinned.

"Not slick enough. Near as I can figure, Carole, Jesse and Derek were all friends in college. Carole and Jesse looked so much alike that they could pass for twins. Carole must have seen the advantage in that. Carole had been stealing hundreds of thousands over a matter of months. Derek got involved somehow and the two of them managed to walk away with ten million dollars without anyone being the wiser."

"Someone must have found out if the FBI was involved," she said.

"Carole realized they would trace the money back to her eventually and needed a way out. Enter Jesse Coleman. Here was a woman that was her perfect match in every way. Except, Jesse had a drug problem, maybe that's how Carole got to her," I said.

Jordan nodded. "I remember the autopsy showed Jesse had high levels of cocaine in her blood."

I stood and looked out onto the porch. "Carole and I made love that night. Sometime later they knocked me out with chloroform, killed Jesse and left me with the body. With Jesse dead and me bringing the news that she and Carole were the same, no one would think twice about trying to find Carole."

"That would explain why the fingerprints didn't match. Damn," she cursed.

"What are you talking about?"

Jordan scooted to the edge of the sofa, her eyes avoiding mine. "Listen, you need to know something before we go any further. The police suspected that there may have been more than one woman involved in this."

"What do you mean suspected?"

She sighed. "Okay, they knew there were two different women involved. Jesse Coleman's prints didn't match the one's Prentiss had on file for Carole. It's common practice to take fingerprints of anyone dealing in securities. After your revelation about Jesse, the police didn't waste any time checking out her prints, but when the ones from Prentiss didn't match, they knew they had stumbled onto something."

"And no one thought to tell me this?"

"The decision was made not to tell you because they still weren't sure how you figured into the equation. You didn't know which woman you were involved with, so we decided to see how things would play out," Jordan said.

"So who was in on this decision?" I asked.

"Lt. Brandon and Nelson agreed it was the right thing to do and, at the time, so did I. I'm sorry if that doesn't make you want to trust me now, but that's just how it was."

"Well, I'm glad you were straight with me, Jordan. I guess we can call it even." I shrugged. "Besides, Carole is still on the loose and probably thinking she's home free."

"You're right, who'd be looking for a dead woman?" She finished her first beer. "Something still bothers me though. Derek. How did he screw up and get caught and not Carole?"

"I think Carole planned to double-cross him from the start. Why else would her grandfather help lead me to him?"

"Well that was stupid," Jordan offered. "Why not just let things run their course and have the police believing you had done it?"

I reached for the other beer now. "I've spent the better part of the day trying to answer that question. She had everything set up right. Why jeopardize everything in a risky double-cross? There was always the chance that Derek could have decided to spill his guts and take her down with him. She was in the clear with all of it, so why?"

Jordan pulled her glasses from her face and studied me silently. I sipped my beer, hoping she would give me some logical reason things had happened the way they did. I waited for her to tell me how Carole could have let me be accused of murdering her.

"Eddie, was she in love with you?" Her voice made me tremble.

Suddenly I remembered that last magical night we spent in each other's arms. I remembered what it felt like to taste her, to feel the hunger in her touch. I remembered her lips upon my skin and how she struggled to tell me what was so hard to put into words. Perhaps in that moment, she had second thoughts about what was yet to come, about how things could be if she chose another course. But was she in love with me?

"I think I know where she is. I'm almost certain she hasn't left the country yet—not without making sure that no one is still looking for the ten million." I replied.

"You didn't answer my question," Jordan said.

"Carole Spenser took advantage of her clients' trust and killed two people in the process. She has to face her crimes," I said. "How she feels about me isn't important."

"You're still in love with her, aren't you?"

"Maybe coming here was a bad idea," I raised my voice.

"Is that why you came here? You're still in love with her I've got to know if—"

"—Yes, dammit!" I yelled defensively. God, there it was and even I couldn't believe I had said it. I was still in love with her. "I'm sorry. You didn't deserve that."

"Don't worry about it. You want another beer?"

I shook my head. "No thanks, I can barely finish this one." I tried to work up a smile and then turned away.

"I don't know if I can trust myself with this alone, Jordan. I know that Carole has to face her crimes. I know that what she did was wrong and she has to pay for it. But there's a part of me that is so damned happy she's still alive. You don't know how I wrestled with trying to find a way to deal with her death, and now that I know she's alive..."

"What are you telling me, Eddie?"

I fixed her with a stare. "When the time comes to do what I know in my heart is right, will I be able to? Or will I only see the woman that I love? That's why I need your help, Jordan. I'm not sure I trust myself. If I can't bring myself to do the right thing, I want you there."

She let out a sigh before answering me. "Don't think that I don't appreciate what you coming to me with this means, but should you have gone to Lou with this?"

"Hell no," I snapped.

"Eddie, at least call Lou and—"

I shook my head. "—Lou would throw me in a cell to keep me away from this."

"And that's bad how?" Jordan asked.

"Have you heard a damn thing I've said?"

"I've heard everything you said, including the part where you don't trust your own judgment where this woman is concerned."

"Look, I know I'm asking you to go out on a limb for me Jordan, but you're all I've got."

When I turned to her again, Jordan was gone. I wondered if she thought everything I'd told her was bullshit, some cock-eyed story to get back in her good graces. But then she emerged from the dark hallway. She had that same snub nosed .38 she surprised me with at Carole's. It was a steel-blue Smith and Wesson with a black handle. She opened a drawer on the coffee table and pulled out a box of ammunition large enough to wipe out half the street. She loaded it carefully, then stuffed the gun and extra rounds in her purse and swung it over her shoulder.

"What the hell are you doing?" I asked quietly.

She grabbed a jacket from a closet. "I've got some friends on the force in Chicago who might help and I can take some sick time tomorrow. We can call them both from the airport, and you can let Lou know what's going on once we get there."

I smiled at her. "In case I haven't said so already, thanks for not shooting me the other night."

She grinned back. "Here's how I see it, Mr. Gideon. Carole Spenser has been a busy girl. She stole ten million dollars, framed you, had a hand in two murders, fraud, and by sheer luck, has kept me from binge-watching *Weeds* on Netflix, again."

She tucked the varsity jacket under one arm. "I'm pissed off. So let's go get the bitch."

TWENTY-THREE

I didn't bother trying to get any sleep. My body, like my gun, was locked and loaded. In my mind I knew what had to be done. As luck would have it, news of Derek Simmons' death and the Prentiss scandal made national news. The FBI, with Fielding's face on every news report, had decided to milk this one for all it was worth.

Jordan contacted the authorities in Illinois and arranged for them to work with us in apprehending Carole and Cappie. While we were in flight, Jordan had the Chicago police check out the retirement community where Cappie lived. It was no surprise to either of us when the report came back that Cappie checked out with an attractive dark-haired woman on his arm.

Jordan had promised me one thing before we left Columbus. Given the way Fielding and his boys screwed up Derek's takedown, I didn't want to involve the FBI until after Carole was in custody. I couldn't handle seeing her get blown away like Derek. I wanted a chance to bring Carole in alive.

"Can I ask you a question?" Jordan leaned over.

We'd tossed for the window seat and she'd won. I was still a little miffed at that.

"You and Nelson, what's the story there? Why do the two of you hate each other so much? Who threw the first punch?"

"I suppose I owe you that much," I smiled. "Believe it or not, it all started with my partner, Nelson's father."

"Nelson's father was your partner?" she stammered.

"Pete was the best cop I knew then. He was everything I wanted to be—caring, tough, street-smart. He knew his way around this town like nobody I knew." I reached into my wallet and pulled out a photo I hadn't looked at in a long time.

"What's this?"

"That's me, Pete, and Lou." I handed her the picture. "Pete took me under his wing after Lou got promoted. Pete was like a big brother to me, always making sure I didn't screw up."

"Sounds like you were pretty close," she commented.

"Like I said, he was like a big brother."

I took the photo and returned it to its resting place. I was usually hesitant to remember anything about that time in my life, even the good days. It hadn't always been painful, not in the beginning at least. Pete taught me a lot about the job: how to read a suspect's face, how to listen to the sound of their voice, observe their body language. In a strange way, Pete made me in part who I was today. Whether for good or bad I wasn't sure I wanted to know.

"So what happened?" Jordan asked.

I glanced out at the bed of billowy clouds we glided over. "Being a cop is like joining a fraternity, with rules and guidelines we follow for the people we protect and for each other. Rule number one is to always watch out for your partner. Pete used to hang out with three or four other cops at a bar on the east side. For a while, I was the errand boy, a twenty-two-year-old rookie. They'd have me grabbing their dinner while he sat in and talked to Forman, Randall, Kelly, and Kirkland. It was like they had their own little club. It took a while but they finally decided to allow me to join them one evening after Pete saved my life," I said.

"What happened there?" she asked.

"We'd pulled this car over. Some guy was driving a little weird so we stopped him. As I walked up to the car, the guy jumped out with a sawed-off shotgun in his hand. I didn't know what to do. The guy must have been high or something because he started yelling and screaming at me and I hadn't said a word. He pointed the gun at me and then he just fell. It took me a minute to realize that Pete had shot him. The guy didn't even look to see if I was alone or not. Pete saved my life." I said.

"He sounds like a great guy," she smiled.

"He was, in the beginning..." my voice trailed off. "Pete was involved in something I didn't want to believe at first. Internal Affairs approached some of us about officers they believed were involved in illegal activities. Pete's name was on that list. At first I thought they were just trying to railroad him, there's no love between cops and IAD. Those of us who weren't on the list were being watched from both sides, everybody was looking for the guy who'd rat out his buddies."

"Wait a minute," Jordan held up her hand. "You mean there were bad cops everyone knew about but no one would turn them in? How could you live with that? How could they call themselves cops?"

"That's the type "A" response the Internal Affairs boys bat around to everyone. You guys think that just because we're cops that makes us some kind of superheroes."

"Isn't that just what you guys want everyone to believe? That you're some kind of special breed above the rest of us lowly imbeciles?" She sneered out of the corner of her mouth. "Aren't you supposed to be better than the rest of us?"

I wanted to tell her where to stick her special breed and use a steel-toed boot to make sure it got there on time. But despite her sarcasm she was here with me because she listened last night.

"Wearing the uniform doesn't give you any special privileges, Jordan." I answered quietly. "More to the point, there are times when the badge is the heaviest weight in the world. Putting it on every day wasn't always easy."

I could see Jordan studying the look on my face, trying to unravel the mystery behind my little metaphor. I could feel a cold flush as her eyes ran from chin to my cheeks. Her concern made reliving the experience a bit easier.

I ordered another drink from the flight attendant before I started again. "I guess you got more than you bargained for."

"I won't know that until I hear the rest of your story," she said softly.

"It was a Thursday night. Pete was a little edgy for some reason. We had stopped to grab a bite when Forman and Randall rolled up. Forman told Pete that there was something going down over on Livingston Avenue so we checked it out. Pete didn't say a word all the way over and I wasn't sure what was going on. Livingston was way off our beat and I knew that Forman and Randall weren't patrolling there, either. We turned our lights down as we pulled into an alley. Forman and Randall closed off the other side."

The flight attendant returned with a cool scotch and water. The scotch was weak, but decent. "We lucked up on a drug deal. Three guys were passing around jokes and jumbo bags of cocaine like it was candy. Pete radioed Forman that we were getting out of the car to approach them. Forman said something about not starting anything without him."

"Anyway, we got out, snuck up on them. As bad as I was shaking, I'm surprised they didn't hear us coming. Pete called out and identified himself. I hit them with my flashlight. They were a bunch of kids. Everybody started running. Forman and Randall had them cut off and two of them still got away. They grabbed the kid who was still carrying the drugs. Forman roughed him up a bit and Pete started asking him questions. He wanted to know where the drugs came from, how good the stuff was."

I took another sip. "I knew something was wrong when I tried to cuff the kid and Pete shoved me out of the way. He said he was handling it. He was in charge. Randall found a bag full of money and started howling like a banshee. Forman took the money and the drugs and threw them in his squad car. They were all laughing while Pete pushed the kid down to the ground and told him to go home and forget what happened. The kid was too cocky for his own good. He started mouthing off that he knew who we were. He'd seen us rip off his friends before. Then he called Pete a pig. Pete took out his gun and shot him," I finished my drink and my story.

"My God," Jordan exclaimed.

"Forman and Randall didn't do a thing. They looked at Pete and then at me. Pete bent down and took a gun from around his ankle and put it in the kid's hand. They left a couple of hundred-dollar bills and one bag of coke."

I ran my fingers against the rim of the plastic cup. "The next thing I remember was being back in the squad car, listening to Pete tell me that we had to watch out for one another, trying to convince me that the kid didn't give him any choice. The son-of-a-bitch even reminded me that he had saved my life. I should remember I'd be dead on the street somewhere had it not been for him."

"So you protected him?" she queried.

"For two days," I recalled. "I couldn't shake the sight of that kid's body lying in the alley. Forman and Randall never turned in the money or the drugs. There wasn't even a report filed about the shooting. It was like none of it ever happened. I knew what they did was wrong, but Pete was more like a brother than a partner. I couldn't bring myself to give him up."

"What changed your mind?" she asked.

"Five thousand dollars," I sighed. "I found it in my locker two days after the shooting. Forman and Randall patted me on the back whenever they saw me, telling how I was turning into a real good cop. I ran into the john and puked. I knew right then that I didn't deserve to call myself a police officer and neither did they. I went to Lou and told him the whole story. Six hours later, Forman and Randall were in custody and they sent a car to get Pete."

Jordan put her hand on mine. "For what it's worth, you did the right thing, Eddie."

"Did I really?" I raised an eyebrow. "When the whole thing came out, I discovered that Pete, Randall, and Forman had been ripping off dope dealers just so they could sell the shit themselves. Pete never went to jail. He blew his brains out in his bathroom when he saw the squad car pull up. He must have known I confessed. Following my conscience made me an outcast. Pete and the other guys committed the crime, but I was ostracized. They passed me around from one cop to another like a bad cold or something. They all had valid excuses; guys transferring, promotions, personal differences, but the bottom line was nobody wanted a snitch for a partner. Cops aren't supposed to rat out other cops. That was the cardinal rule, and I broke it."

"Nelson blames you for his father's death," she surmised.

"Nelson blames me for a lot of things. Pete's suicide just tops the list. He's publicly accused me of framing his father and the others, trying to build a case on me for longer than I care to think about. To tell the truth, I really don't think he's qualified to be a DA. He's got guts like his dad. I just wish he'd get off my back." I shifted in my seat, feeling the hours catching up with me. "So what's your story, counselor?" I mused.

"Well, I'm the third youngest Assistant D.A. in the city's history. My father and all my brothers are all cops. I have a brown belt in Tae kwon do and I clean my own gun. My last boyfriend turned out to be a flake, so I let him think he dumped me just so he wouldn't come running back a month or so later. I'm a decent cook but I love a good hot dog."

"So why didn't you become a cop?" I asked.

"I had no desire to sit around the dinner table and compare battle scars with my brothers. And I really don't like uniforms. Y'know, Eddie—"

"—Gitz. My friends call me Gitz."

She smiled. "Alright, Gitz. You know that Carole and her grandfather may have already left the country. They could be a thousand miles away by now."

I leaned back into my seat. "I'm betting that Carole wants to make sure we still believe she's dead. I think I'm beginning to understand her. She's far more patient than Derek. That's why I had you call your friend at the newspaper. I want Carole to see the story on Derek, let her think that she's in the clear. That's when she'll know it's time to leave."

A flight attendant approached us with a phone and passed it to Jordan. I listened with jaws locked as she coordinated with the Chicago authorities. This betrayal business didn't sit well with me. I had a sickening feeling in the pit of my stomach. Is this what it was like for Cassandra when she found out about my affair with Jacks? God, no wonder she'd become so bitter and vicious towards me.

"Sir, please fasten your seatbelt. We'll be landing shortly," the attendant smiled.

Jordan pushed a button on her phone and laid it on her lap. "I talked with a Detective Johnson. He'll meet us at O'Hare. Get this, a woman rented a car yesterday and brought it back to the airport an hour ago. She paid in cash and tipped the clerk fifty bucks for being nice."

I raised an eyebrow to her. "Yeah, and?"

"Her name was Jesse Coleman."

TWENTY-FOUR

The weather in Chicago was bright and sunny. A morning haze had just begun to lift and a few light wisps of dew lay everywhere. The sweet smell of jet fuel and Illinois smog left a delightfully foul taste in my mouth. It was nine-twenty in the morning, and the butterflies had again taken roost in my gut, like little earthquakes shaking the life out of me.

Detective Johnson met us at the gate as promised. He was a fair-skinned Black man who bore a slight resemblance to Rev. Jesse Jackson. He was tall and sported the shadow of a beard he kept neatly cut. Two plain clothes officers flanked either side of him. Behind him in the distance, there was a gathering of state troopers, local cops, and a few fellas from Cook county sheriff's department.

"McCrae, Franklin county D.A.'s office," Jordan introduced herself.

Det. Johnson shook her hand. "Your brother described you to a tee, Ms. McCrae. My men and I are at your disposal."

"You guys know each other?" I asked.

"Not personally," Johnson answered. "I came through the academy with her brother, Joey. He asked me to tell you that you haven't been back for a visit since Christmas."

"Sorry, this is Eddie Gideon, he's working with me. And you tell Joey that the phone works both ways." She cut back quickly. "What have you got so far?"

"The rental car was returned at 7:14 this morning." His voice had a striking resonance. "We had TSA triple-check security and delayed thirty-three passenger flights while we searched passenger lists and check-ins the last two hours. The only flights that have left between now and then have just been cargo hops. No one has purchased any tickets under the names of Spenser or Coleman, and no hits on face recognition either."

"They're probably holed up in a hotel close by," Jordan surmised.

"We're already working on that. I've got a couple of guys checking all the hotels, motels, and rentals in the area," Johnson replied.

"She wouldn't go to a hotel, probably something low key and unassuming," I threw my two cents in.

Jordan was quick to back me up. "He's got a point. They've got to be really careful with ten million in cash."

Johnson sighed. "There are maybe a dozen hotels close by, over 400 in Greater Chicago, plus around 6700 Airbnb listings. We're on it, but it's a lot to sift through."

I looked up at one of the monitors displaying the arrival and departures scheduled for the day. In my gut I knew Carole was close. I could almost smell the scent of her perfume in the air. Jordan had me wondering whether Carole might've already gotten away. She could have had someone else bring the rental car back.

But I couldn't think that way. If we lost her now, we'd lose her forever. I had enough guilt in my life to deal with without this. I owed it to the two women who didn't deserve to be murdered so Carole could spend the rest of her life sipping Mai Tai's on a beach somewhere. That's when

I saw it. A flight delayed, but cleared, now departing at 10:45 to Miami; with a change of flights to Barbados, the Virgin Islands.

"Hang on. She's still here. What about that one?" I pointed. "What are the possible connections once it lands in Miami—within say four hours?"

Johnson pulled up a flight list on his phone and scrolled for a moment. "Austin, Barbados, Boston, Havana, London, Nashville, Panama City—there are over a dozen..."

"You find something, Gitz?" Jordan slid up next to me.

"Where do you buy a ticket around here?" I asked Johnson.

"C'mon." He led us down a busy corridor with the whole police team in tow.

I got the feeling Johnson tolerated me only because of Jordan and her brother. He stayed just ahead of us while Jordan and I exchanged curious glances. Johnson flashed his badge at the woman behind the US Air ticket counter.

"Can I help you?" She looked at Johnson nervously. She must've assumed the worst based on the number of cops that converged on her tiny space.

"We need to check your passenger list for the Miami connecting flight to Barbados, Jessica," I read her name tag as I stepped forward.

"We're looking for two people. A man and a woman traveling together under the name of Spenser or Coleman," Jordan showed her ID to Jessica.

Jessica nodded and began working her fingers furiously against her keyboard. All eyes were upon her as she stopped and ran her finger against the screen in front of her. There wasn't a smile among the group of officers, which seemed to make her that much more nervous.

"I'm sorry, but I don't show anyone listed on that flight with either name," she said.

"Are you sure? Can you check it again?" Jordan inquired.

Jessica typed some more. "I'm sorry, there are no Spensers or Colemans listed on that flight."

"Dammit," I slammed my fist against the counter.

"Gitz, I'm sorry." Jordan put her hand on my shoulder. "They can't have gotten far. We can still catch them."

"I was so sure." I turned away from the counter.

"My team will continue checking the flights." Johnson patted me on the shoulder.

I stormed past the herd of cops and stared out at the jets waiting to haul and dump their next load. Carole would soon be one on of those planes if she wasn't already. Laughing at how she manipulated the hell out of us all, especially me. I punched the glass, striking it several times before Jordan grabbed me.

"Calm down!" she urged. "You're gonna get yourself some alone time in Cook county if you don't get a grip."

"How can you expect me to be calm when Carole's about to walk away scot-free and I know I helped her!" I snarled.

"You didn't know she was alive."

"I should've known! I should've been smart enough not to let my emotions get in the way of my job," I gritted my teeth to keep from shouting. "I should have been able to see when someone was pulling my chain, instead of just losing it the whole time."

"You mean like you're doing now?" she grinned.

"What the hell is so funny?"

"You," she snickered.

I tried to stay mad, focus my anger. But Jordan's smile hit me like a flame against a sliver of ice. "What about me?"

"Look at you. You've got all the earmarks of a jilted lover. You're irrational, loud, and reactive. You're making a complete ass of yourself," she laughed.

"Jordan, don't hold back. Tell me how you really feel."

She exhaled. "Look, I'm just as upset. But all this pounding and screaming isn't going to help us catch Carole. Just take it easy, okay?"

I laced my fingers together and threw them over the back of my head. I was suddenly aware of all the looks we were getting from the cadre of cops behind her. "I see your point, counselor. I did act like an ass."

"C'mon, let's get some coffee." She led me by one arm. "God, if this is how you react to your lovers, I shudder to think what you might have done if you had been married."

"Yeah, me and Ca—" I stopped dead in my tracks. "What did you say?"

"About what?"

"If we had been married," I recanted.

I bolted back to the ticket counter as quickly as my feet could carry me. Jessica braced herself as I slid before her again. "I need you to check on that same flight for anyone named Gideon."

Jordan and Detective Johnson huddled around me again. I looked over and saw that Jordan had her fingers crossed, whispering prayers as Jessica began punching her keyboard again. Carole had used Jesse's name to rent the car, so why not use another name to keep suspicion further away from them?

Jessica's face glowed. "Yes, yes. A Mr. and Mrs. Edward Gideon listed on the flight to Barbados."

My heart leapt into my throat.

"I'll be damned," Johnson said.

***

The Macasaway Motel was just a stone's throw away from the terminal, a dirty brown, two-story complex made up of about thirty or so units, all squeezed together next to another motel and a fast-food place. Mr. and Mrs. Eddie Gideon had taken temporary residence in one of the lower units while they waited for their flight. Safe in the knowledge that no one knew who they really were. We planned to change all that. In less than an hour, we had moved into the units on either side and above them. The sheriff's men had the area sealed off and filled the parking lot in front of the motel with undercover cops. It all came down to a waiting game now.

I finished my third cup of coffee as I leaned over a parked car. I stared at the room, not having said a word to anyone since we tracked them back at the terminal. The only person I wanted to talk to was Carole. She alone could tell me why all of this had happened. Before they took her and her grandfather off to prison, I had to know why she did it.

Jordan leaned over the car, binoculars in hand. "They're still inside. Our guys can hear voices through the walls. I'm giving Johnson the go ahead to move in on them."

"Why?" I inquired.

"Gitz, she's there. We've got them. I don't want to draw this out any longer than I have to and we want to bring her in alive." She kept her eyes focused on the door. "You asked me to be here to help you make sure Carole was apprehended. I'm doing just that."

"What about our deal?" I raised my voice. "You said you'd give me a chance to talk her in."

"I'm sorry, I can't." She tried to face me. "Look, for what it's worth, we'd have never gotten this far without you and I'm glad you were right.

But I won't risk your life just to give you a moment to hash out your problems with your old girlfriend. What if you went in there and they took you hostage—or worse?"

"She won't," I replied.

"But what if they do?"

"Then you blow me away with them," I said.

She shook her head. "You're crazy. No way Gitz, we take her down right now."

"Dammit, you owe me!" I pointed sharply. "She'd be halfway around the world by now if not for me. You wouldn't even know she was alive if I hadn't come to you. Don't cut me off like this, Jordan. You owe me!"

"Alright, for God's sake!" she yelled. "If you're so hellbent on doing this who am I to stop you, right?!"

I didn't bother to answer.

Reluctantly she waved Johnson and two of his men over to us. Jordan drew a deep breath as they crouched beside us. "Bernie, you're not going to believe this. We're sending Mr. Gideon in to bring them out."

He stared at her. "You gotta be kidding."

I handed her my gun. "Let's just do this."

"You're going in unarmed?" she asked. "At least wear a vest."

I waved off the vest too. I wanted Carole to believe I was on her side.

"Tell me this isn't how you guys do things in Columbus," Johnson moaned.

"No, Bern. Have your guys walk him up to the door," she ordered.

"Save the escort for when I come out," I said.

She reached out and squeezed my hand. "You get hurt and I'll kill you."

"I know," I smiled. "Thanks, Jordan." I moved around to the front of the car.

"Gitz," Jordan called out. "If you're not out of there in ten minutes, I'll do what I have to Eddie. I mean that."

I took a deep breath and I made my way across the parking lot to the door of Carole's motel room. I didn't know whether to kick the door in or jump through the window. I listened to hear what they were doing inside and then, I just knocked.

I listened again to the sound of footsteps approaching.

I was surprised Carole didn't ask who it was before she swung the door open. She had changed her hair again, sporting a blonde wig and blue contacts, but it was Carole. She wore a dark pair of slacks with a black shirt tied in a knot in front. My voice failed me as we both stared at each other in disbelief. For a time we stood there, speechless.

"Eddie?" she stuttered.

"Can I come in?"

She stepped back, never once taking her eyes off of me. I could feel my heart in my throat as I shut the door behind me. We stood there frozen for a moment in time, neither of us believing in what we saw, both so overwhelmed by what we felt. Before I could speak, she rushed into my arms. Suddenly the reasons for finding Carole didn't seem important anymore. I had found her again. God, it felt so good to hold her after all this time. As I breathed deep the smell of her wig, I prayed this was all some crazy dream. A nightmare that had its way with us and was about to end. But reality had a way of jolting you when you least expected it.

Carole pulled from my embrace unexpectedly, pushing me away as she reached for a suitcase on the bed. I could see the money packed neatly in rows. She stood erect again, holding a gun.

"Dammit Gitz, why did you have to come?"

"You didn't leave me much choice, Carole. Did you think after all I've been through I wouldn't try to find you?" I spoke gently.

"No Gitz, don't you understand? We can't be together anymore. Everything's changed." She drew down on the sights of her revolver.

"How has it changed? Make me understand! How could you be involved in this?" I pleaded with her.

"Just go! Leave and forget you knew me!" she shouted.

"I can't! Do you have any idea what you've put me through? I thought you were dead! I've been ripping myself apart believing that I let someone come in and kill you. Do you know what you did to me?" I didn't try to hide my rage.

"Caroline? Everything alright?" A voice called from the bathroom.

Carole turned sharply. It was Cappie. He'd been in the shower and hadn't heard me come in. Carole tensed, her face becoming hard and emotionless. For the first time I saw a face of someone quite different from the woman I still loved.

"How did you find us?" her tone sounded dark.

"Mr. and Mrs. Gideon?"

She smiled. "That's my fault, I suppose."

I shook my head. "I can't let you take all the credit. Derek gave me a hint before he died. And after I made a call to your former college, things started to add up. Even Cappie slipped up without either of us realizing it. He said he was happy that I was with you when you died. How would he know that? Unless he'd already knew I'd be coming to see him."

She looked stunned. "You found me just from that alone?"

"There were a few other things that helped me find you—your letters, the check from Jesse to Derek, the 911 call you made, Joan Richards, even the picture Cappie gave me by mistake. But I didn't put it all together until I got your college yearbook."

She stared at me. "Congratulations, you've solved the crime."

"Carole, it's over," I held out my hand. "The police have surrounded this place. You can't get away. Turn yourself in."

"And go to prison for murder?" she laughed out loud.

"Derek killed Jesse and Kelly."

"Derek was a dumb prick. I shot Jesse."

I stood there in shock. I had always believed Derek had done all of the killing, seemed more his style. Not once did I ever suspect that Carole may have killed Jesse. Even now, the thought seemed too much to bear.

"You?" I stammered.

She held up the gun and gave me a fierce and burning look. "I had to shoot her. You didn't know Jesse like I did. We used to be like sisters. She was my best friend." Carole moved toward the window. "Things didn't have to turn out the way they did. All she had to do was go along with the plan. But you had to know Jesse, she didn't like not having a hand in anything we did, even if it meant she'd get paid big time. We never meant to kill her at all. But Jesse got a little too greedy for Derek and me. She was already an addict, after she let some creep get her all strung out. When the time came, I realized I was doing her a favor."

"By killing her? Some favor."

She turned to me again. "Yes, I killed her, what else could I do? She was still my best friend, and a part of me hated doing it. But she would've spoiled everything we'd worked for. All those years kissing ass at Prentiss, and for what?

"Are you nuts?" I asked. "I know people who would've died to be in your position at Prentiss, Carole. You didn't have anything to cry about. You were making it."

She waved the gun at me. "No, don't you see Gitz? Once you've had a taste of making that kind of money for someone else, it isn't long before you want some of your own. My contract with Prentiss kept me out of the real game. I'd spend and make a million dollars a day and none of it was mine. Why should I settle for six figures a year when I could have so much more?"

"But murder?" I stammered.

"She was dying anyway," she said indignantly. "I did her a favor, Eddie. I took all the pain away."

"So Jesse was an addict. But how can you call killing your friend a favor?"

She stared at me, blankly. "I set her free."

In that moment something clicked, like a charge moving through my mind. Suddenly all the illusions I'd clung to, my saintly image of Carole, simply faded. I no longer saw the woman I once loved, just a sad and desperate shell of someone I once cared for. And perhaps, for the first time, I really knew who Carole Spenser was.

"And what about Kelly? What did you set her free from? My God, she was just a kid!" My anger twisted my gut.

"Don't you think I know that?! Don't you think I would've done anything not to let Derek kill her?! He said she overheard us talking and that she went to you. He was determined to stop her and I couldn't stop him," she began to fall apart.

"And what about me?" My voice softened as I drew nearer. "Do you remember what you said to me that night Carole? Do you remember... 'Can we believe in fairy tales, can love survive when all else fails?' Did I imagine that or was it real?"

"My... heart...belongs...to me," she whispered.

Finally, she let the gun drop to her side. Carole pushed past me and moved slowly around to the head of the bed. She sat down and held the gun in her lap. She was quiet, almost withdrawn. I had touched a part of the woman I once knew. Somehow I had to convince her to give herself up.

"When Derek suggested we find someone to frame for the murder, I thought it would be easy," she tried to smile. "I told myself that I wouldn't let myself get too involved with you, that I'd keep things in perspective. But then I got to know you and be with you. I was ready to deal with a jerk—the kind of cocky asshole that usually hangs out in Deacon's. I never believed you would be so kind to me. I didn't know how to handle that. Why did you have to be so damn good to me? I never dreamt I could fall in love with you."

"Is that why you double-crossed Derek?"

She nodded. "Despite everything I've done, I never wanted to hurt you."

"But why Carole? What was worth all of this?"

She wiped her eyes and composed herself. "I had two reasons. One, for the money. Two, for the pain."

"Pain?" I stammered.

"Is that so hard to understand?" Tears stained her cheeks again as she looked toward the bathroom door. "The one person I'd do anything in this world for is my grandfather. I love him more than life. He raised me, put me through school. He's done everything to give me a good life. Why would I do anything less for him?"

"The ten million, you stole it for him?" I asked.

"For the both of us," she exclaimed. "I needed an out from Prentiss and I owed him the luxury of spending his last days with me, happy and at peace. I would do anything to make him happy Gitz, anything," she hissed defiantly.

"Even murder?"

Cappie emerged from the steamy bathroom. "You mean the death of a thief and a drug addict? I'd hardly call their untimely demise murder, Mr. Gideon. But my granddaughter is a very loyal child."

He possessed a strong stride—not the frailty I'd seen in him—it was all a part of his act. He wore a new suit. A cream-colored two-piece that covered a tropical shirt. He had obviously dressed for a trip.

"Nice suit," I commented.

"Thank you, dear boy," he brandished a gun and slapped me across the face. "You have indeed proven to be the proverbial thorn, Mr. Gideon. I applaud you for being a credit to your profession. I still don't understand why she chose you. Then again I suppose it would've been hard to frame someone decent. But you have the look of a man who's been in jail."

"All that just from the color of my eyes," I said.

He slapped me again.

"Cappie, stop it!" Carole cried out.

He went to her and put his arm around her. "There now child, I didn't hurt him all that much. I just had to show him who's in charge. We respect each other now."

"What the hell do you know about respect? Tell me Cappie, how could you allow your own flesh and blood to do this, just for you?" I rubbed my jaw.

"I suppose there's no harm in telling you that, Mr. Gideon," he smiled. "Like dear Jesse, I too am somewhat ill. My doctor told me I have less than six months. The cancer in my stomach will soon eat away at me and I'll be a hair's breadth from the grave. That was four months ago, but I still feel fine. I'll feel even better once you help us get out of here."

"You won't be going anywhere, Cappie," I leaned toward them. "There are about thirty cops and a dozen feds waiting to see me walk out that door in a couple of minutes. And if I don't, I'd lay odds you won't make it to your first shuffleboard game."

"They won't shoot if we have you," he grinned.

I grinned back. "You don't know Jordan Taylor McCrae. She doesn't give a damn how many holes she has to put in me to get to you. You won't get ten feet past the door."

"Bastard," he snarled.

From the look on Carole's face, he intended to shoot me. Anger lit up his face like the Christmas tree at the White House.

I could tell he was starting to lose it from the way he bit down on his lower lip and rushed back to me. I had lost count of the minutes and prayed that I'd been there for more than the ten Jordan allotted me. I prayed really hard.

"Cappie wait, what are you doing?" Carole called out.

"I went along with your little plan because I love you, Caroline. But I can't stand the sight of this thing anymore. I'll walk out with him and you get the car. They won't shoot."

"Don't listen to him, Carole. You try something crazy and you're dead, both of you."

"Shut up," he sneered.

"I get the feeling you don't care for me that much, Cappie. Tell me something, what is it about me you despise so much? Something about the way I kiss your Carole not to your liking or doesn't the idea of us being intimate agree with you?"

I tried to force him to make a sudden move. He smacked me across the side of the head with his gun. I fell backwards into an end table before I hit the floor. The angle of the fall caused me to rip the stitches in my chest open. Damn, I was getting tired of getting the shit kicked out of me. Cappie played right into my hand, doing what I hoped he would, acting nuts and getting careless. Common sense reminded me that he who has the gun makes the rules. I just tried to keep playing along.

Cappie turned back to Carole, her eyes still filled with tears. He put his arms around her and rocked her gently, trying to calm her down. Then he came back to work on me. His backhand caught me just above the right eye. Blood spilled into my eye, partially blocking my vision. Damn, where the hell was Jordan?

"Caroline, we don't have many choices left to us," he hissed. "Your lover has forced us into a very difficult position."

"He's right Carole, eventually you're going to have to shoot me. You don't have much choice, right Cappie?" I struggled to my feet. "Is this the kind of love you were talking about, Carole? The man who claims to love you, ready to kill the man you've fallen in love with? What kind of love is that?"

"I told you to shut up!" Cappie pointed his gun at me again.

"I don't swim in the right social circles? My income too low? What is it, man?" I stared at him as best I could. "A pity though, imagine what could have been if we were all one big happy family. Or ain't I good enough, Cappie?"

"Your kind could never be good enough," he snapped back.

I wiped the blood from my face. "My kind? Which kind would that be?" I could see the rage burning in his eyes and the mounting fear on Carole's face. "Well which is it? Am I too poor or something else?"

"Eddie, stop this!" she pleaded.

"Y'know I understand now why you cried every time we saw that movie, Carole. You weren't just like Sara Jane, but maybe your mother was. Was it her dream to be something that she wasn't or your grandfather's? Tell me if I've got it right, Cappie. None of your ancestors worked in the fields, right? You found a way to pass for white and thought nobody would ever hold you down again. Tell me Carole, was your father like me? A dark-skinned Black man? Someone your grandfather was ashamed to have as his son-in-law?"

"Shut up!" Cappie sneered.

"All the things Cappie did for you—sent you to the right schools, introduced you to all the right people. Maybe he saw in you a chance to succeed where he failed with your mother." I egged him more, trying to buy myself some time, hoping Jordan would come crashing through and end all this. But if I couldn't get my little gambit to pay off soon, I'd be losing more than my balance.

Cappie leaned in on me, seething. "Why is your kind always so eager to tear us down, Mr. Gideon? Am I wrong for not wanting to see my granddaughter end up like her mother, running off with any common trash that came along? You self-righteous niggers!" Cappie shouted. "Always running around like the world owes you something instead of getting off your lazy asses and getting it the way we did!" Cappie kicked at me. "I don't owe any allegiance to the Black race. Your kind has persecuted me as much as any other has, so don't come at me like I'm some goddamned Tom. You're the reason why I had to pass, and I'll be dead before another of you has one of mine."

"I don't give a damn about your hang-ups, Cappie. You made your bed, why drag Carole down with you? Do you get your rocks off using your granddaughter?" I raged back.

"Shut your filthy mouth!" he took aim at me. "Black bastard, I'll kill you myself!"

"No, stop it!" she grabbed for his gun.

I tried to blink away some of the blood. My blurred vision kept me from reacting quickly. I tried to rush Cappie, use my weight to force him down, but my movements were slow and sluggish. I reached out, trying to get my hands on Cappie before he could gain control. I swung at what I thought was his face and missed by a mile. Bam! The gun went off, the bullet striking me in left shoulder. I felt it cut through muscle, lodging against the bone in my arm. The pain made it so damn hard to think.

I could hear Carole struggling harder with Cappie now, and I prayed she'd get the best of him. I knew I had to get out of the room before he could fire again but between my head and the bullet in my arm, I wasn't sure I could escape. I rolled down to the floor again, trying to get my bearings and scooted along the wall.

Bang! Another shot rang out. The shot rung in my ears and my adrenalin rushed through me like fire. I forced myself up on my knees, holding my hand over my gunshot wound. My arm had started to go numb and the gash in my head throbbed. But I was alive.

I squeezed my eyes together tightly two times and my vision came back, though only slightly clearer. Carole stood alone in the center of the room, her chest heaving up and down sporadically from her fight with Cappie. Her mouth hung open as she stared down at him. He lay on floor at her feet with an eerie stillness. Cappie didn't move and as near as I could tell, he wasn't breathing. His gun was still in his hand. I managed to get up and kicked it away. Carole seemed oblivious to all of this. Her face was blank and empty.

"Carole?" I called to her.

Finally she screamed, realizing that in their struggle she had killed her grandfather.

"Cappie!"

"Carole Spenser! This is the police! Come out with your hands up!" Johnson's voice thundered over the loudspeaker.

"My God, I killed him," she stammered. "I killed my grandfather. I killed Cappie."

I fell back against the wall, trying to keep from passing out. My legs shook as I tried to stay upright. It hurt to breathe.

"Carole, listen to me," I panted. "The police are going to come through that door any second. Put the gun down and come over here."

"God, I killed him. I killed them all," she sobbed.

"Carole, there isn't time. Put down the gun," I pleaded.

She stood erect, trying to get control of herself once more. Carole turned to me, her cheeks red and eyes swollen from crying. She shook her head as she drew closer and surveyed my condition. Her hands trembled as she reached out toward me.

"All this trouble over one woman," she laughed. "Is this all that's left? No Cappie, Jesse...Derek...Kelly? Just me and this gun?"

Her eyes focused on the revolver. "I'm sorry for everything I put you through Eddie Gideon, I truly am. I guess I just got so wrapped up—all that money. But I didn't want you to get hurt, Eddie. I never felt for anybody the way I feel for you." She leaned in close and pressed her lips against mine. "God, I love you so much."

"Carole I—"

She cried, "Hush baby, I know. It wasn't our time."

I found myself frozen as she turned away from me, walking toward the bathroom. My mind said go to her and take the gun out of her hand, but my body wouldn't respond. My legs didn't have the strength to move. Suddenly shotgun butts pounded the door. The police were screaming and coming closer to us. I guessed ten seconds were left before they would burst through the door. I turned back to Carole again. I could see the bullets fall from her hand. Why didn't she just drop the gun?

"Carole?" I called to her again.

She turned and smiled at me, her eyes glistening with tears. She held up the gun, pointing it at the door. The hinges of the door buckled under the police's assault. I managed to brace myself on my good arm. I pushed up the wall but my head was swirling. The dizziness began to overwhelm me. Despite the pain, I kept trying to get to her to grab hold of the gun.

"Goodbye, Eddie." Carole held the gun tightly with both hands "Goodbye, my love."

"Carole, no!" I reached out to her just as the door swung open.

"Bang," she whispered.

The room came alive with gunfire.

I never reached her in time.

EPILOGUE

All but $100,000 was recovered from the money Carole Spenser swindled from her clients. Despite that, everyone at Prentiss was happy with the outcome. Nelson Peters was still miffed at having another chance to get even snatched from him. But he kept his complaints behind closed doors due to all the attention the D.A.'s office was getting, thanks to Jordan.

I tried for weeks to locate anyone related to Jesse Coleman and turned up nothing. The thought of her nagged at me. I didn't know her at all but no one should die alone and forgotten, with no one to grieve for them. She deserved better.

I spent the next few days in the solitude of my thoughts, bothered only by Rita bringing me dinner, or John, who on occasion would sit with me quietly drinking a beer. I spent a few extremely memorable days with my kid. When left to my own devices, I found myself thinking about Carole and Cappie. I couldn't completely put them out of my mind. I still ran across the picture of the two of them every now and then, never remembering where I laid it last, always forgetting to throw it away.

In the days that followed, I attended Kelly Greer's funeral and met her family. Like most of us, Kelly's family didn't know how they were going to pay for the services. Fortunately, someone had made an anonymous donation to the family. And though it couldn't equal their loss, it more than covered the cost of all their expenses. A donation in the amount of $100,000.

E.G.

ABOUT THE AUTHOR

James Moorer is originally from Cleveland, Ohio and a proud alumnus of THE Ohio State University. He's a best-selling author, screenwriter, literary manager, publisher, actor, producer, and director. He specializes in dark, character-driven horrors and thrillers where the road to hell is paved with good intentions, where the good fight is more than an ideal, and where blood-covered heroes love pancakes. He lives in Los Angeles and enjoys weekends cruising the coast with his wife, Venita, while searching for the best brunches in Southern California.

www.jamesmoorer.com

ACKNOWLEDGEMENTS

The character of Eddie Gideon, hard-boiled private investigator, was born in Columbus, Ohio. Thank you to the people and the city itself, who played no small part in creating this story.

From my collegiate partners in crime, Steve Butler and Kimberly Fuller, who sat through my wild imaginings in Dr. Stewart's class at The Ohio State University, to the fraternal brothers Curtis McGuire and Tyrone Montgomery, Sr., who listened to me ramble over far too many beers and shots of whiskey—thank you all!

A special thanks to the men and women of the Columbus Police Department for their valuable insight and experience.

Finally, I must acknowledge all the great detective novel scribes who showed me the way with their own works. Your words and worlds will live with me forever.

JM

ALSO BY JAMES MOORER

Black Bones Jones: *Ex-Slave. Ex-Soldier. Exorcist.*

In late 1865 the Civil War is over, but an evil is sweeping across the South. Fearing his small town will be next, an Arkansas sheriff employs the help of Black Bones Jones—an ex-slave, ex-soldier, and exorcist—to save all he loves.
(fiction: horror, western, supernatural)

www.ingramcontent.com/pod-product-compliance
Lightning Source LLC
Chambersburg PA
CBHW011853300726
48970CB00009B/2782